T0368197

Pandemic Dreads:
An Unfinished Manuscript

GENARO J PÉREZ

PANDEMIC DREADS: AN UNFINISHED MANUSCRIPT

Copyright © 2024 Genaro J Pérez.

All rights reserved. No part of this book may be used or reproduced by any means, graphic, electronic, or mechanical, including photocopying, recording, taping or by any information storage retrieval system without the written permission of the author except in the case of brief quotations embodied in critical articles and reviews.

This is a work of fiction. Names, characters, places, and incidents are either the product of the author's imagination or are used fictitiously, and any resemblance to actual persons, living or dead, business establishments, institutions, events, or locales are entirely coincidental.

iUniverse books may be ordered through booksellers or by contacting:

iUniverse
1663 Liberty Drive
Bloomington, IN 47403
www.iuniverse.com
844-349-9409

Because of the dynamic nature of the Internet, any web addresses or links contained in this book may have changed since publication and may no longer be valid. The views expressed in this work are solely those of the author and do not necessarily reflect the views of the publisher, and the publisher hereby disclaims any responsibility for them.

Any people depicted in stock imagery provided by Getty Images are models, and such images are being used for illustrative purposes only. Certain stock imagery © Getty Images.

ISBN: 978-1-6632-6010-9 (sc)
ISBN: 978-1-6632-6011-6 (e)

Library of Congress Control Number: 2024901950

Print information available on the last page.

iUniverse rev. date: 02/23/2024

FOREWORD

Several summers ago, to defray the cost of my tuition in college, I worked for a demolition crew in the French Quarter in New Orleans. As the crew was removing the debris from the remains of a house, one of the workers found a box filled with papers. The house was located in the South East corner of Saint Ann and Bourbon. It had been the residence of a retired professor who had worked at the University of New Orleans for many years. The entire block of houses, covering Saint Ann, Bourbon, Orleans, and Royal, were leveled to build a hotel. Since I was the only "college boy" on the crew, the box of papers was given to me to dispose of. I took the box home and discovered, among other items, the typescript which follows this introduction. Moreover, under the manuscript were numerous sheets of carbon paper that had been used and depicted the trial of Clay Shaw. I have not changed anything from the manuscript written with a typewriter on onion paper. I have published the manuscript as is with all the grammatical errors and tried to keep it as the author (authors?) left it.

The manuscript is a collection of stories within a biography and autobiography. The author at the same time claims he is writing the biography of an acquaintance—he is also writing a great deal about himself. The text is filled with allusions to world-known writers by name and with numerous intertexts of their works. The creator was studying English at LSU in Baton Rouge and there are many allusions to the University, the students, and the town. He is very familiar with the Quarter and many of its inhabitants. Some of the book's sexual descriptions are very graphic and many readers will have a very negative reaction because of it, and yet, the depiction of some of the characters reflects a very careful character study of the subjects. The author claims to have been a chef at several Quarter restaurants for which I have not been able to find documentation. I also have been unable to find records about the subject of his biography: Tulane does not have the family in question as one of their founders. One must conclude then that the character in question never existed. LSU also does not have a record of that person attending the University. The apartment in Saint Ann, however, has a record of its owner living in one of the apartments and was assassinated during Mardi Gras while wearing a drag queen's outfit. The man who killed him was a well-known anti-gay activist. The owner of the building was from North East Louisiana and came from a very prominent Acadian family. After he passed away, a corporation took over the rental of the building. I was not able to discover anything else related to the names that appear in the text. For instance, the two professors were the parents of the female, Mia who appears towards the end of the text. It will be up to the readers to determine whether the manuscript is fiction or biography. The pandemic, of course, as depicted, has never happened. The influenza virus at the beginning of the twentieth century, notwithstanding its mortality, was never so deadly. The manuscript ends abruptly and I did not find anything else related to it in the box.

Tobias Alexander Robichaux

His name was Frederick Honoré Peters, IV, and he was the end of a long line of physicians that extended from mid-eighteen century New Orleans. Some of his ancestors had an essential role in the creation of Tulane Medical School. I was fortunate enough to meet Fred at Louisiana State University in Baton Rouge when we were English majors. His family is an example of the "American Dream," whereby you attain privilege as a product of hard work. (The silence outside is thunderous). I dropped out of L.S.U. in my second year and started working as a waiter in "The Court of Two Sisters." I had rented an apartment in Fred's building without realizing he owned the place and had Hibernia Bank manage it for him. It was astounding when we met each other on the stairs one afternoon. We became closer than we were in Baton Rouge as a result. Shortly before the Pandemic broke out (1990, or thereabouts), a jealous husband assassinated Fred in front of the building.

I held his hand as he was expiring, and he asked me to take care of his manuscripts and gave me the keys to his beautiful apartment where I am now writing. I am using a new gadget, an IBM selectric typewriter, that allows me to erase typos without having to use that white liquid, which reminds me of vomit. But, I am talking too much about myself and not enough information about Fred. I am trying to write his biography using the information in his apartment: some of his unfinished and unpublished writings. Fortunately, I can have the New Orleans Public Library at my disposal without anyone around: most people in the world have died. We didn't know what the virus was at first when millions were dying in a matter of forty-eight hours. Corpses covered the Quarter rapidly like an afternoon thundershower. I remained indoors and removed the bodies from the building, wearing the kitchen gloves used by dishwashers and an old plastic raincoat that belonged to Fred, and began the arduous task of removing eight bodies from the building. A couple of the apartments were empty, who knows where they passed. I have lost track of time, so I do not know how many months (?) have passed since the outbreak. I was meticulous at first, remaining indoors, and not venturing out. Still, as the hum of the Quarter disappeared (in a matter of weeks?), I ventured to the grocery store on Royal and removed anything to eat I could stow in the apartment without the need for electricity—which was out worldwide (?).

After several weeks of recoiling into the building, I decided to explore the Quarter not only to see how things were but also to exercise. Fred's apartment was not big enough for the daily run I took before contagion overpowered humanity. The very few scientists left have been unable to find how the virus behaves. It is related to smallpox, but the vaccine for smallpox many people had taken as children is not preventing people from the infection. A hypothesis is that the survivors have a mutation in their DNA that immunizes them against pox (a genetic super code?). Actually, I do not believe that pox is the correct term since the victims have no sign of pox. Their bodies are relatively untouched by the virus: people were dying from all the future flaws in their organs: heart, kidneys, pancreas, etc. A scientist indicated that it was a very poetic/elegant death—no suffering. "The Rest In Peace Virus," as it was known. The person ill wanted to go to sleep wherever they were and, when they lie down, they never got up. He was not taking into consideration all the accidents resulting from conductors, drivers, pilots who passed while flying, and all the people perishing as a result.

The stench outside was unbearable. I had been using Fred's incense and became adapted to the different scents. On my first trip to the store (so long ago!), I found many candles and incense sticks that I had brought to the house. The streets were poke marked with decaying bodies, so I covered my nose with a bandana and inserted some mentholatum ointment into my nostrils.

But I digress. My intent is to write about Fred whom I feel deserves some sort of tribute for all the good and the evil he did. I am going to be quoting a great deal about his forebears from some of his writings. The following is taken from his short story "Sans Mercy":

"During the War of 1812, after the Battle of New Orleans, which took place in present-day Chalmette, my great-great-grandfather, Frederick Henry Peters, who was a British physician with the 14th Light Dragoons, was taken prisoner and placed in a cell in a building in what it is today the Court House in the French Quarter. Food and water were brought to him by a young creole that was no more than seventeen at that time. He was allowed to leave the imprisonment after three months, stipulating that he would return to Great Britain immediately.

However, being a physician was an asset to the men who governed the city. They found a law that stated that a foreigner could obtain permanent residency if he married a Louisiana citizen. My great-great-grandfather decided to marry his warder since he had nothing in Great Britain. His jailer was beautiful and made love, unlike any British woman he ever had. Oshun was young, lovely, and had a French mother and a biracial father with Cuban roots. Her parents were financially independent and had an herbs shop in the Quarter that sold the best honey in town. Most of this information I have taken from family albums and the family history, carefully written by a family member every generation, and some newspapers from those years available in the family library—mostly writing about Mardi Gras. Oshun's parents were well provided by their shop. The family was well-liked and tolerated by the upper circles of New Orleans's society. Her father had a very interesting ascendance; he was born in Cuba, and his Catalan mother had married an African physician."

The rumor at the time was that the special ingredient of the honey was a small amount of

Cannabis Indica that provided the relaxation its consumers loved. During the pandemic of yellow fever in NOLA in the 1850s, it was said that the honey helped deal with the "stranger." The victims would start to bleed through their eyes, nose, and ears and would vomit partially coagulated blood. The acclimated people were the survivors: Fred's family was, evidently, of a fascinating DNA composition that prevented the virus from harming them. (Un)acclimated were those who succumbed to the plague—much of this information I received from Fred in Baton Rouge, where I met him. On Thursdays, he would invite a group of friends to his beautiful apartment a couple of blocks from campus on Dalrymple Drive. There we smoked weed until someone took the floor and began to talk, with occasional interruptions for clarification or other relevant questions. The invited group researched a favorite author and discussed it. Fred was captivated by writers such as Lucien Goldman, Sartre, and others. I found some Goldman notes that give me a better insight into Fred's character. Goldman was a prestigious writer in the sixties when Fred read the Marxist writer. Fred saw himself as a tragic figure who was self-analyzing very frequently. His promiscuity, he believed, resulted from his wanting to realize himself in the other: women.

There are about a hundred people left in the Quarter. After we had taken care of the crowded streets, we checked houses to remove the corpses from homes. Most people seemed to have the imperative of going to bed once the virus infected them. It was an elegant death: they went to sleep without blood, without vomit. We divided into groups and went to every house to remove the corpses. A sign was posted outside the home, indicating the place was empty. We also borrowed an excavator and several trucks from a construction in Esplanade to take the corpses to Jackson Square, where we dug giant holes in the green spaces where we deposited the carcasses. Unfortunately, some of the survivors in the houses were not exposed to the virus until we came along and infected them. After that, we took precautions to keep those people inside their homes. The virus seemed to be in the air, in everything we touched. The result was deadly for those we came into contact with the virus. Those who had remained in their homes all this time did not have the idiosyncratic DNA. All of us on the troupe (we felt sometimes we were the actors in a surrealist play written by a mad playwright) had the immunity. Obviously, if we came close to those still hiding in the buildings, we would cause their deaths.

Once all the homes in the Quarter were visited, we began to scrutinize the hotels. The job seemed unsurmountable at the time, but what else did we have to do? The group had an arrangement: the teams surveying houses or hotel rooms were the owners of everything in that space. It was a payment for removing corpses and taking them to the street to be pick-up by the trucks and taken to Jackson Square. It was a heavy task dealing with decomposing corpses who seemed to melt upon the touch. Their stench, which penetrated the masks, made me vomit regularly. We began excavating with front end loaders deep pits in four grassy areas of Jackson Square. The final outcome looking from the adjacent roofs, seemed an enormous Microsoft logo. Four giant square pits forming a larger square. When we excavated to a profundity of ten feet, we stroke water. At that point, we began to deposit all the corpses from the houses and hotels in the pits. The Mississippi is drying up and the trickle of rain we get daily is not enough to replenish it. Fortunately, the water from the river is not breaking through the holes as expected.

One fascinating thing I noticed about the group, although logical, was that most members were gay. Since many gay people live in the Quarter, it would make sense that the group's composition would have such a majority. And yet, I wondered if the DNA of gay people was more prone to natural immunity to the virus. Three Septuagenarians in the troupe were given de facto control of the unit in recognition of their experience and familiarity with the group. They had resided in the Quarter for decades and knew everyone. Everyone in the Quarter was known by their nicknames: In the case of the three leaders known as Your Honor, Profe, and Pato.

But I digress. While in Baton Rouge, when we were very stoned with various chemicals (some with mushrooms, others with chemicals and synthetics, I preferred Colombian Gold cannabis.) I knew an instructor in chemistry at L.S.U. who grew it very carefully--for a few generations at this point. Fred would stand and recite fragments of poems. Other attendees would imitate him, and the scene became a living theatre. I never had the nerve to do anything like it, but I enjoyed it tremendously. He recited, with a very poignant voice, the Emily Dickinson poem, "I am nobody! Who are you?":

I'm Nobody! Who are you?
Are you – Nobody – too?
Then there's a pair of us!
Don't tell! they'd advertise – you know!

How dreary – to be – Somebody!
How public – like a Frog –
To tell one's name – the livelong June –
To an admiring Bog!

These *tertulias*, as Fred called them, continue when he moved to the Quarter. Fred took French and Spanish so that he was conversant in those languages and he read quite a bit of literature in those areas. He read a great deal without having to depend on translators that often were not natives of that particular language and made "horrifying" errors, according to Fred.

During one of those participatory sessions, a dozen years later, Fred became very agitated and started reciting one of Supertramp's pieces, "The Logical Song." His voice was very masculine and could hit highs and lows with little effort. When he recited a poem, he somehow knew when to go high and when low:

When I was young, it seemed that life was so wonderful
A miracle, oh, it was beautiful, magical

But then they sent me away to teach me how to be sensible
Logical, oh, responsible, practical

Then they showed me a world where I could be so dependable
Oh, clinical, oh, intellectual, cynical

(Oh, won't you tell me) please tell me who I am
Who I am, who I am, who I am

Once Fred reached the verse "Please tell me who I am," he would use a falsetto to articulate his sentiments about the question. Most of the attendees were never able to rival Fred's performance.

From such a soiree, I learned that Fred had some psychological problems resulting from his upbringing. His mother had aborted a baby boy before Fred was born, and the pregnancy with Fred was brutal to the point his mother could not have children anymore. Fred did not consider himself the eldest son. After his first attack of sentimentality with his first cat, he overheard a conversation between his parents. This attack gave his parents examples of a hypersensitivity they felt was a handicap.

At the time, he was five or six years old. His best friends were a calico cat, an aunt (his mother's sister) had brought him from North Louisiana, and Bona, the housekeeper. The cat became the love of his life. He did not have any friends, and, although he went to a very select kindergarten, the other children (except for birthday celebrations) he did not associate with him. Perhaps his parents did not want him to associate with people who did not belong to their class. The pre-school accepted only Tulane faculty and some distinguished people from the New Orleans community. Thus, his only friends were his cat and Bona, the housekeeper who took care of the house and all the servants. Bona was an octoroon. She was born in Puerto Rico to a Hispanic mother and an African father. His father had been born in Haiti and claimed genealogical descent from royalty. She came to New Orleans with her mother when she was a little girl and went to a Catholic School in Crescent City. She became a polyglot thanks to the language classes she took in school. She could speak English, Spanish, and French, which helped Bona secure a position of hostess at several Restaurants in the Quarter—from "The Court of Two Sisters" to his last and better-paying work at "Antoine's." How she became part of Fred's household is another story he describes in one of his short stories.

One day, while playing in his enormous backyard, Fred heard a squealing of breaks. His cat appeared, running toward him and collapsing with a tremendous amount of blood dripping from his mouth as he expired. Fred began to scream, collapsing, his body overpowered by tremors, and Bona called the family doctor, who gave him some sedatives. His father and mother were out of town attending a professional conference. The entire episode was highly harrowing for the little boy whose psyche was wounded.

The Society of Jesus, the Jesuits, is a distinguished religious order of the Catholic Church and was founded by Ignatius of Loyola in 1540. New Orleans has one of the best Jesuit schools in the U.S.A., and Fred was fortunate enough to attend there. The Jesuits are considered the mavericks of the Catholic Church. Throughout history, they are well known for championing controversial causes. The most recent controversial stand was related to "liberation theory" concerning many Spanish American countries.

Fred started the second grade at Jesuit High at the age of six. At four and five, he had several tutors who prepared him for the second grade. Bona had already started teaching Fred Spanish and French, which gave him an advantage at school regarding languages. The manuscript I am reading does not indicate the date on which Fred was informed he would be attending Jesuit High. It was during dinner in spring 1950. His father told him that following the family tradition, shortly after his birth, the family had registered him on the "list." Jesuit High kept families interested in their son's attendance at the school in such register. He had been admitted and would start in the fall. His father continued with information about the Jesuits and his incredible time at the school. How Fred remembers the event suggests it was a traumatic event. He was not comfortable with other people around, and he dreaded attending Jesuit High. Fred decided to investigate the school and asked Bona to help him. The encyclopedias available at home gave a fascinating portrayal of the Order: they were rebels as Fred saw himself.

Fred distinguished himself during the years he spent at Jesuit. As expected, the emphasis of his studies had been science until he arrived in the twelfth year of high school. There he met Father Xavier Arizabaleta, and his perspective of the world changed, and he, along with it. Father Riza, as he was known by the students, had a Ph.D. in Philosophy and Literature from Princeton and took Fred under his wing immediately. He gave Fred copies of books in the *Index Librorum Prohibitorum* to read, which surprised Fred immensely. He read Sartre's *Nausea*. He read Marx and Lucien Goldman's "Marxism in crisis," where Goldman criticizes the inability of Marx to reach the masses. Fred also decided that authenticity, from an existentialist perspective, was a purpose for which he would strive.

There was much information/disinformation about the Jesuits to which Fred was exposed. The power of the Superior General (the Order's structure reflected the military background of his founders) was legendary since he was more powerful than the Pope. Hence the moniker: "Black Pope." It was said, among elementary students, that a tunnel extended from the classrooms and office buildings (a five-floor structure that stretched for half a block) to the two-story building where the priests had their suites and many study rooms. The tunnel went under the gym, the football stadium, and several tennis courts. To be invited to go there indicated the priest, in particular, wanted to seduce the student. Fred discovered this was totally false. Notwithstanding the pedophile scandals of priests in other orders, the Jesuits were not accused of sexual abuse by any student during the time Fred attended.

Father Arizabaleta invited Fred to go to a meeting in the other building. The priest gave him a permission slip to go through the tunnel. He went to the basement, and there was a white door with a sign stating: "Entrance for those with permission only." He entered the tunnel, very well-lit with white walls with religious images. There was an image of the Sacred Heart, the Virgin Mary (Mother of the Society of Jesus), Saint Ignatius, and many other photos I could not identify (oops! I keep changing the narration to the first person—which is the result of reading Fred's diary). There were biblical citations: 1 Kings 14:24. "And there were also male cult prostitutes in the land. They did according to all the abominations of the nations that the LORD drove out before the people of Israel." The Jesuits' motto was ubiquitous: *Ad Majorem Dei Gloriam.* After a long walk, he entered the other building, where a brother asked for his permission slip and where he was going. Fred proceeded to father Arizabaleta's suite, whereupon, after his knocking, the priest opened the gothic door (The doors to the suites had different looks!), greeted him and took him to a meeting room. These meeting rooms were on all three floors adjacent to most suites. They had a chalkboard, and several chairs, which Fred saw, as he walked to his destination. Fred also recognized some math students listening to a priest (a math teacher) write a few mathematical equations on the board. Fred realized it was very advanced mathematics, for he did not recognize the symbols. Father Riza began to talk about Sartre and the existentialists—something he was very interested in understanding the concepts. He did not, he felt, have enough information during class time. Father instructed him about existentialism and, particularly, Christian/Catholic existentialism. It accepted the presence of God in the universe rather than the Godless concepts of Sartre. Bad faith (*mauvaise foi*) was something he deemed very important since he strove to be authentic. Father Riza, however, accentuated the catholic/Christian aspect of the philosophy, which he considered an indirect style of Christ's teaching. The meaning of parables, for instance, depended on each individual to confront the significance on his own. According to father Riza, there were four essential tenets: individual, God, being, and truth. The awareness that one is born and during life, the individual creates his essence. A building, in contrast, has its essence (blueprints) before it is constructed. Fred read Kierkegaard's *Fear and Trembling*, and he learned the horror of life and the difficulty of achieving authenticity.

The result of Father Riza's teaching (to some extent recruiting) made Fred morose, and he wondered how he could achieve authenticity. Bona asked him what troubled him, and he replied that he was considering becoming a priest. Two weekends later, when his parents were out of town, Bona had a surprise for him: the two most dissolute nights in his life. While he slept on Friday night, Bona appeared in his room totally nude and with a red candle whispering strange words. She entered the bed and began kissing and fondling his body. Fred had several orgasms that night.

In the morning, he was awakened by one of the two teenage maids Bona hired to clean around the house—Delfina.

As Fred regained consciousness from a night of dissoluteness, he was overcome by the scent of sea shells--a marine fragrance engulfed him. Delfina was at that moment kissing his penis, Bona came in with a breakfast tray, and the other maid, Lillian, was there too. The three women were nude, and their vulvae were gleaming. The two teenagers had a violet streak separating the dark downy. In Bona, the stripe was so dazzling crimson that it looked like she had half a grapefruit between her legs. In his drugged state, Fred thought they had vertical smiles. I suspect they were frolicking with each other before I woke up. The three women's toes were manicured and painted red, and Fred, in his semi-consciousness, thought they were fifteen strawberries for his munching. Bona fed him coffee and toast with a lot of honey (he discovered later that the honey was laced with cannabis). The dishes were put aside when he finished, and the three girls got in bed with him. Fred was still naked from the night before, and, to his surprise, he had an erection. He did not think he could get another erection so soon after Bona had given him so much pleasure the night before. The two teenage maids were young and attractive creole girls. One of them had blue eyes on her brown face. The young girls' growing breasts were budding tomatoes ready to be gobbled. The callipygian girls had, as well, bright red nipples that stood up in attention and tasted like honey; their *panocha* was salty—sea salt. They "devoured" Fred for hours until Sunday when he fell asleep. *I am not sure if I should copy the images/narrative of the sexual acts written by Fred. As I read his diary, I encountered a number of paraphilias I did not know existed (Did I tell you I took some psychology at L.S.U.?)*

His parents arrived Sunday afternoon, and his father woke him up for dinner. Fred realized as he awoke that he could never be a priest. The room was clean, and he was wearing his pajamas, so his father did not see anything amiss when he went upstairs to his room to awaken him. Fred went to the bathroom and discovered his penis was bloody, and so was his underwear. His testicles shrieked in agony with every step he took. While he took a shower, he felt his anal area smarting as he lathered himself. His penis felt raw, bleeding, and swollen—it looked like a red and pink suckled lollypop. As he dried himself in front of the wall mirror in the bathroom, he noticed his body covered with scratches and bites. His big toes were purple, swollen, and faintly bitten, and so were his lips.

It should be noted that Bona kept the young maids for two years. She trained them and located better employment with higher salaries for the girls. She felt her duty was to help women of color enhance their living by assisting them in finding better jobs. They were creole women from the Bossier City area. There was a case of a young woman Bona felt was bright enough to attend a university. She did all the necessary bureaucratic paperwork for her to attend Loyola University. The young woman graduated and became a very successful teacher.

Your Honor, Profe, and Pato turned out to be the perfect organizers. Pato has been sent to the U.S. to study by his father to discontinue the constant harassment his homosexual son was enduring in Costa Rica. The "tico" youth did very well in Loyola University and became an accountant for JAX beer. At this point you are wondering how I am in possession of so much intimate information. I will explain: My freshman year at L.S.U. was very pleasant and I met Fred that year when he was a junior. By then, he already had had his trauma with the calico. I managed to work my way through two and a half years of college as a busboy during the summers in the Quarter. I am an orphan and have been working in this life since the age of fourteen. The Department of English was respected still for the number of distinguished southern novelists and literary critics that walked the halls, imparted concepts in those classrooms. I wanted to be a writer, not a critic, so left the school after two years and one semester. My working in the best restaurants (Antoine's, Brennan's, Galatoire's, Arnaud's) located in the Quarter allowed me to have a large number of acquaintances in very high places. Pato was also a legend during Mardi Gras because he spent a great deal of funds on his drag queen costumes. He has received several trophies throughout the years to show for it. Your Honor was involved in the Garrison prosecution of a few gay men the D.A. maintained were involved in the assassination of J. F. K. He worked for the New Orleans Civil District Court—421 Loyola Avenue. Profe was a professor of Sociology at the University of New Orleans and was also a gay man living in the Quarter. Unlike Pato, he was very discreet about his escapades. I saw him a great deal because many of his meetings were conducted at dinner time.

After all the houses and hotels were emptied of bodies and all the corpses were buried, we took a census and our home or areas we claimed in the Quarter. The structure of our living conditions began to be developed. We had been saving the pets from the homes of the dead and had started to develop a system to deal with them. Two committees of three Quarterites would take care of cats and dogs. Stations for feeding and fresh water were established. The dogs committee was tasked to remove from the Quarter aggressive dogs. All entrances were barricaded with the help of the construction that was taking place when the pandemic started. It seemed the "visitor" squashed most of humankind. The construction site had excavators, bulldozers, dump trucks, fork lifts, front end loaders, and a myriad of machinery with which I was not familiar—fortunately there was an engineer among the group of survivors. There were now only four entrances to the Quarter: Clockwise starting with Bourbon at twelve, Saint Peter at Three, Royal at six, and Saint Phillip at nine. All the entrance through the other streets had been blocked and some of the survivors had chosen to live on the buildings adjacent to the blocked streets. We used most of the cars in the Quarter and all the detritus we could find to blockade the entrance to our kingdom. We also have a great deal of gasoline from all cars which allow us to take the trucks we had on patrols. We seldom found other humans. There were a few enclaves that wanted no association with other humans.

Most utilities were disconnected, perhaps for the rest of our lives, so we had to conserve the fuel from all the autos we were using to block all entrances. Our first attempt to contact people from outside ended in failure. About a year ago, we sent a squad of three on a pick-up with our best firearms. They never returned. There were three or four guys who had disappeared. During our weekly meeting, we do a roll call. Those are the only casualties during the year or two (I no longer have a calendar) post-pandemic. So, we fear we are not ready to confront whatever is beyond the Quarter into the hinterland New Orleans is now. The several enclaves we knew about have disappeared—we no longer encounter them when we go on patrol. We had gone beyond Woolworths, Holmes, and Maison Blanche and had crossed Canal Street to search for available fuel and food. We did not know what to expect when we went into the stores. As was the case when we entered new buildings and residences, we found a lot of corpses which we interred in the boulevard part of Canal Street. The grass and flowers grew there, and we could excavate their graves on the soft earth. We reinforced all the canal entrances of the stores facing Canal Street with their rear at the Quarter. We found enough in these stores to satisfy the needs of the ninety-five persons who were left. The ninety-five comprised 50 persons over 60 and 45 under 60, and sixty males and 35 females. Among the females were several lesbians and several widows. The males were a mixed bunch with hetero/homosexuals and bisexuals. Two young females of about seventeen had been staying with a High School teacher who passed to a better life. The young girls were beautiful and wild. They became a source of controversy and division, leading to our establishing rules.

The girls, Hebe and Sage (names given to them by the Latin teacher), had been kept by this high school teacher who owned a house in the Quarter. The teacher kept them on drugs—Spanish fly (*cantharidin*). The drug has strong scents: musk, citruses (orange, lemon), kaffir lime leaves. Because of the treatment they received from the Latin teacher, the females were going through a sexual crisis that catapulted them into a reckless stunt. They decided to ingest some of the Latin teacher's pills, undress, and walk the streets of the Quarter nude, offering themselves to the few pedestrians they encountered. The young women were detained after several men had intercourse with them. Two lesbian couples volunteered to deal with them—do the specific intervention. They kept them locked in different rooms and different houses to isolate them. Two lesbians were nurses, so they had psychology training and knew how to deal with them. The event was the topic of several meetings. It was decided that the first Tuesday of every month would be free love day. Those individuals who wanted to make love would walk around the Quarter naked, ready to give and receive. The first few months, it was wild, but after that, only the under forty still participated.

The event of the girls with the drugs surprised me since whenever we cleaned houses in the past, I was known for requesting all drugs and cash found in the place I was cleaning. If the other person I was paired with disagreed, I would be assigned a different partner. I received some recognition and preference among the group, so getting my way was not too difficult. The drugs I had found were many, in addition to grass and horse. I had the good fortune to find a dealer's home who was a pharmacist and knew the market very well. He had plastic baggies filled with pills, and each bag had a tag with the pill's slang name. The following are some of the downers, uppers, etc. I had collected: Blue Bullets, Blue Birds, Blue Angels, Blue Dolls, Green Frog, Green Dragons, Rainbows,

Pink Ladies, Black Bombers, Brownies, Pink Hearts, Rosa, and Lightning—a brief sampling. I had not used any of them yet, since I was satisfied with Fred's large stash of grass.

It has been three years (?) since the start of the pandemic, and there have been quite a few changes in leadership and the structure of the Quarter government. Profe and Pato have passed to another hell, and a widow in her sixties who was a school teacher assumed the administration. There has not been a dramatic change in how we conduct our lives. We have sent out patrols as far as Kenner, but there is no sign of living beings. The positive outcome of our ventures outside the Quarter was the number of groceries and fuel we found throughout our areas. We found generators which made our lives much more pleasant. The outcome of exploring Metairie and Kenner has resulted in our adding to our stockpiles of food since the supermarkets we found had plenty of food, fuel, and many other exciting items. I am collecting cash, and everybody gives me all the dollar bills they find. I have at home a closet filled with dollar bills and other oddities (sex toys with very imaginative dildos) I have discovered in the many residences we have visited. The beauty of some of the mansions is still there. The luxurious furniture varied with the mood of the room; their pantries filled with cans, grains, and dried fruits; the closet full of clothes that changed its contents with the seasons; the myriad of details that underscored "privilege." We have determined that there are other small enclaves.

In the Tulane area and Algiers across the Mississippi, unknown groups do not want to communicate with other humans. These communities warned strangers from coming too close to their territory. I have been one of the explorers--a group of twenty of the youngest "quarterings." I have participated in most of the surveys we have undertaken. As mentioned, we have gone from west Canal Street to Canal Blvd to the best-looking mansions in Metairie. We now go out more often, two or three times per week—if it is not raining. We have turned several houses in the Quarter into warehouses where the residents can pick up any household needs and, frequently, the unusual item such as coffins.

It has been three years (?) since the start of the pandemic, and there have been quite a few changes in leadership and the structure of the Quarter government. Profe and Pato have passed to another hell, and a widow in her sixties who was a school teacher assumed the administration. There has not been a dramatic change in how we conduct our lives. We have sent out patrols as far as Kenner, but there is no sign of living beings. The positive outcome of our ventures outside the Quarter was the number of groceries and fuel we found throughout our areas. We found generators which made our lives much more pleasant. The outcome of exploring Metairie and Kenner has resulted in our adding to our stockpiles of food since the supermarkets we found had plenty of food, fuel, and many other exciting items. I am collecting cash, and everybody gives me all the dollar bills they find. I have at home a closet filled with dollar bills and other oddities (sex toys with very imaginative dildos) I have discovered in the many residences we have visited. The beauty of some of the mansions is still there. The luxurious furniture varied with the mood of the room;

their pantries filled with cans, grains, and dried fruits; the closet full of clothes that changed its contents with the seasons; the myriad of details that underscored "privilege." We have determined that there are other small enclaves.

In the Tulane area and Algiers across the Mississippi, unknown groups do not want to communicate with other humans. These communities warned strangers from coming too close to their territory. I have been one of the explorers--a group of twenty of the youngest "quarterings." I have participated in most of the surveys we have undertaken. As mentioned, we have gone from west Canal Street to Canal Blvd to the best-looking mansions in Metairie. We now go out more often, two or three times per week—if it is not raining. We have turned several houses in the Quarter into warehouses where the residents can pick up any household needs and, frequently, the unusual item such as coffins.

I am now on the Cat Committee, as well. I am surprised it took this long for me to be appointed. After all, Fred's Calico was now a well-known figure. She was one of many calicos Fred owned, and, typical of calicos, she was very bright. I provided her with a cat door to go in and out of the house at will. She has invited other cats since the entrance area of the building has food and water. She would be out during the day and at night, but early in the morning, as I woke up after a tumultuous sleep, she would be staring at me at the other end of the bed. She had accepted my presence and the absence of Fred. She has had a large following of friends who seemed to get along very well. Since I was on the Cat Committee, I discovered that the cats were not reproducing. Most of the feline population in the Quarter was spayed and neutered. But we allowed cats to enter from the outside. We felt that strange dogs should not be allowed to enter our enclave.

But I digress. I wanted to give a portrait of Fred before publishing some of his unpublished and published work. Fred, from a very early age, was socially conscious. Perhaps it was a way to transfer his hypersensitivity to cats to humans. In my five semesters at L.S.U., Baton Rouge, I took some psychology, philosophy, and quite a bit of English literature. The department of English was one of the most distinguished in the nation and had a few of the "Fugitive Group" on its faculty. Robert Penn Warren had left a few years before I entered L.S. U. I digress. I have been reading enough psychology books and a great deal of fiction (the New Orleans Public Library belongs to me) so that I can write about Fred. When he was just a junior at Jesuit, he received the proverbial clarion call from the civil rights movement.

During the 1960s, New Orleans was a center for activism. Civil rights protestors used nonviolent tactics such as lunch counter sit-ins, store boycotts, marches, and other demonstrations to call for equality. Fred participated in the efforts that led to four young girls integrating previously all-white elementary schools. I found a paper clip that appears to describe the event and mentions Fred as one of the participants:

On September 9, 1960, seven local university students staged a sit-in at Woolworth's department store located at 1031 Canal Street to protest the store's refusal to serve Black people at the lunch counter. According to *The New Orleans States Item*, this protest was "the first organized demonstration of its kind in New Orleans." [1] The New Orleans chapter of Congress on Racial Equality (CORE) organized the protest and all seven protestors were CORE members.

Protesters included five Black students and three white students--Jerome Smith of Southern University, Ruth Despenza of Southern University, Joyce Taylor of Xavier University, William Harper of University of New Orleans, Hugh Murray Jr. of Tulane University, William Harrell of Tulane University, Archie Allen of Dillard University, and Frederick Honoré Peters, IV, Jesuit High School. Woolworth's employees refused to serve the students when they sat down together at the lunch counter. The students remained seated at the counter while waitresses continued to serve white patrons.

Crowds gathered to watch the protest. Store officials closed and barricaded the lunch counter, but the student protestors remained. Meanwhile, over forty police officers patrolled the store and surrounding area. District Attorney Richard A. Dowling ordered the students to leave the lunch counter, but they refused, and Dowling ordered their arrest. New Orleans Police Officers, under the direction of Superintendent Joseph I. Giarruso, arrested all seven protestors. Newspaper coverage of the arrests detailed the protestors' names, age, school affiliation, and home address.

Fred was a junior or Senior in High School when he started his socially active life. Fred always sat at the back of the public bus and was arrested several times. His father and the family attorney bailed him out. Fred did not need to employ the New Orleans public transportation since he owned a 1958 or 1959 Ford Thunderbird. His father realized Fred would not stop his civil rights engagements, so he suggested Fred keep the attorney's business cards in case of future confrontations with the police.

One of the most absorbing aspects of Fred's character was how paradoxical it was. While participating in the struggle for civil rights, he would go to all the balls and parties during Mardi Gras and take advantage of drunken southern bells. I have gathered all this information from his diaries. He relates that when he was thirteen, he almost perished due to drinking a large amount of alcohol during the carnival. Since then, he did not drink and discovered that during the balls, teenage girls attending them drank too much. The adolescent females were easily tempted by someone as charming and known as the heir to the Peters' fortune. Most of the gowns the women wore had the Mardi Gras colors: purple, green, and gold.

Fred describes his Mardi Gras seductions as a hunting game: women were the prey, and Fred the hunter. He customized the back seat of his T-Bird into a bed. The rear windows had shades Fred could pull down when parked in the darkest area of the Ball or party's parking area. He would attend several balls/parties looking for his quarry: a female showing manifestation of intoxication. Fred then would initiate a conversation to determine her state of mind. The next step would be to invite her to another party, take her to his car, and have intercourse. He never used condoms, and Fred was fortunate not to have contracted sexually transmitted diseases during those years. Most of the females were virginal or did not have many partners in the past. They seemed not to remember the encounters, and if they did, they feared Fred's distinguished name: Peters.

Fred's life in High School was a dolce vita. He managed to breeze through his classes and had the time to be a predator during weekends, Mardi Gras, and other holidays. Fred was a monk in his approach to studying Sunday night through Thursday night. Fred confesses in his diary that he fell into temptation the night before the SAT exams and did not do well enough to merit entrance into an Ivy School. However, Fred was a legacy student at Harvard because of his father and grandfather. The men in his family always did their undergraduate work, premed, at Harvard and their Medical School at Tulane. During this time, Fred was reading Nausea and the concept of authenticity fascinated him. Ergo, Fred felt he would be acting in bad faith if he went the legacy route and deprived someone, among the underprivileged classes perhaps, of entering Harvard. Fred thought that he would be behaving "inauthentically" if he were to prevent someone with better scores from being accepted at Harvard. If he wanted to be authentic, he could not do that.

In his journal, the pages that describe these years (Jesuit High to LSU) are filled with quotations from *Nausea, Fear and Trembling*, and *Steppenwolf.* The following is a selection: "I exist because I think . . .and I can't stop myself from thinking." *Nausea*, ND, 1959, p.135. Fred considered sex to be the meaning of life--a necessary causal being. The following citation perhaps guided him onto that conclusion: "To exist is simply *to be there*... I believe there are people who have understood this. Only they tried to overcome this contingency by inventing a necessary causal being." (*Nausea*, ND, 1959, p.176). "[…] nothingness was only an idea in my head, an existing idea floating in this immensity: this nothingness had not come *before* existence, it was an existence like any other [. . .]." (*Nausea*, ND, 1959, p. 181.)

From Kierkegaard, I found a few interesting entries: "But Abraham believed, therefore he was young; for he who always hopes for the best becomes old, and he who is always prepared for the worst grows old early, but he who believes preserves an eternal youth. (*Fear and Trembling*, (New York: Double Day Anchor, 1954, p. 33.) Fred was fond of the conception of "divine madness," which he felt he underwent frequently. All the readings from the philosophy and literature classes he began at the Jesuit School, and were fully assimilated at LSU, were duly noted on his notebooks.

I will continue selecting items from his journal to provide an interpretation of Fred's character. His inability to adapt to social norms and his decrying the absurdity of life became an obsession. I am citing some more excerpts that accentuate some of Fred's characteristics. Like the knight of faith, the only thing that could save Fred in that last year at Jesuit High was the concept of the absurd. Fred rationalized, too, that through a teleological suspension of the ethical, his behavior during Mardi Gras would not be rape.

Fred considered me to be an example of the Self-Taught Man of *Nausea*. We ran into each other years later at his maternal uncle's Saint Ann's building since I rented an apartment there. He invited me to one of his tertulia's in his uncle's apartment (before his uncle was assassinated during a Mardi Gras by a homophobe). During the talks, he discovered I had continued reading, "educating myself," he condescendingly articulated it. That discovery was sufficient for his giving me the sobriquet Self-Taught Man. We began then the second stage of our friendship. During our "tertulia's," as he called them, I realized Fred's enthrallment with existentialism. I remember frequently hearing the following articulations: "Existence before Essence," "The Encounter of Nothingness," "freedom after despair," "Reason is impotent to deal with the depths of human life," and so on. Most of these pronouncements were peppered in his speech during the *tertulia's* and on his writings.

I am alone most of the time. There are fewer people than before. I seldom find anyone to talk to; I am now going out further into Gentilly and Elysian Fields, and there is no sign of humans. The smell of death covers New Orleans and its surroundings like a shroud. The Quarter, perhaps the entire world, has been overtaken by the pong of decaying violets. Low dark clouds pressing upon the Quarter and the combination of fog and light rain daily contribute to a dreary existence. The Mississippi is almost dry, and humans and ships remains appeared, adding to my realization that the end is near. So many strange things have been taking place that I should stop writing about Fred and provide more autobiographical information.

It is ironic and astonishing that the last days of my life find me residing a few doors from where my mother deposited my newly born body on the steps of the Sisters' of Saint Ann. The sisters have a grammar school and orphanage on Saint Ann Street. She left me at the front door one cold January day in 1943. Mother rang the doorbell, and Sister Angelica saw my mother run away as she opened the door. I have found it fascinating as well that the sacred house of Marie Laveau is located a few doors down. I was a very good and intelligent boy, and I stayed with my first adoptive family from the age of two until I was eight. Unexpectedly, "mother" became pregnant, and a little boy was born. The family decided there was no room for me there anymore. Since I was not legally adopted, the family took me back to the sisters when I was about seven. They left a very detailed character study. The bottom line was that I was college material and should be sent to a school that would prepare me for it. I was attending Jesuit High on a scholarship the father assigned to the convent, father Rafa had obtained for me. So the subsequent foster family would have me attending a good school. The next foster family had me for about a year.

One night, I was awakened by a shadow touching and kissing my chest, and I felt the lips on my deformed penis (the result of forceps cutting into my genitals as the doctor was pulling me out). The shadow grunted as it discovered my deformity and left the room. Two days later, I was back with the nuns. Father Rafa heard my confession and realized those people were deplorably preying on the innocent. Father Rafa spoke with Sister Angustias, the convent's prioress, and they found me shelter while I attended Jesuit High. (It should be noted that father Rafa eventually managed to have a stricter evaluation of the Foster families). My fifteenth birthday was the beginning of my independence. I moved to a rooming house in the Quarter, and worked as a busboy in "The Court of Two Sisters" (affectionately called "two sisters.")

I had two hours to read and study before I went to bed. I did not work on Sundays, so I visited art galleries and museums, went to the movies, and engaged in all the pastimes a child of that age usually engages in. I was always very structured in my life. That is my nature, my *raison d'etre*. Sex did not appeal to me; my only interests were reading philosophy and literature and French and Spanish cuisine. When father "Riza" approached me as he did with Fred about two years before, I could have accepted since monastery life appealed to me. However, the idea of becoming a chef and even having my own restaurant was a dream for some time, and I decided to follow something other than that priestly path.

Days followed one another like drops of water on a bucket. It drizzles most of the year with a persistent snow dribble in January and December that shrouds everything in leprous white--"Mother Nature's leprosy." The days are very cloudy--the clouds have emasculated the sun. Everyone has lost the ability to reproduce. Cats, dogs, and all animals have died. And so have most of the humans I have been associating with in the Quarter. We do not socialize and tend to avoid each other. I have two people I still mingle with and go out searching for provisions and other humans. We have gone through Gentilly and Elysian Fields with no sign of human beings. Still, we found quite a few treasures: food, generators, gasoline, bottled water, drugs, sex toys, etc. Among the animals' casualties was Fred's calico cat: I found her on his bed dead for some time. I only use Fred's apartment to get stoned and look through his books. When I saw that beautiful calico cat sleeping on the multicolored bedspread, I could not help myself and decided to pet her. I realized she had passed when there was no reaction to my presence. Cats and dogs have died, and their birth rate was rare. The same happens with humans: no baby has been born in the Quarter since the Pandemic overwhelmed the world. We were not infected, but the virus caused abnormal manifestations in humans and all other members of the Animal Kingdom. I never had any pets as a child, and my lack of empathy about the extinction of every domesticated and wild animal is the result. The horror of it! As a matter of fact, I don't miss humans much, either.

One of the two young men, Louis and Eddie, with whom I used to go scavenging, died due to the car races they performed on Elysian Fields. Eddie was ahead on his way to the ending at UNO when he lost control of the T-Bird and flew over the boulevard, landing in the middle of it with a massive explosion. This event, in part, ended my teaming with anyone to go on jaunts around the state. I realized that going alone was the best way to explore and discover possible clues as to where, if any, colonies of humans had been established. I was interested in finding shortwave radios, any type of communication device. As I walked outside, dark clouds with the light rain clicking on the street like an old typewriter greeted me.

Six or seven years have passed, and the number of humans in the Quarter has decreased quite a bit. Suicides are the primary cause of the number of casualties. In my notes about my life, I wrote that thanks to father Rafa, I graduated from Jesuit and was accepted at LSU. I had accumulated a great deal of cash from working at the restaurant, so I was ready to pursue my second love: creative writing. I was pleasantly surprised to discover that the School of Home Economics at LSU offered food science, preparation, nutrition, and wellness courses. I had developed a good reputation among the Quarter restaurants, so I had my choice of jobs the summers I came back to New Orleans to work. After two years and a semester, I decided to quit LSU and start working again full-time in the Quarter. It was also an opportunity to get in the kitchen and seriously consider my going from waiter to chef as I had been promoted from busboy to waiter. Waitressing was an enjoyable and rewarding experience since I had the opportunity to meet New Orleans upper class.

Furthermore, the tips allow me to travel for at least one month in the summer to Paris, where I matriculated on a three-week course on culinary arts. The classes in Paris and my visits to the kitchen allowed me to secure an assistant chef job at Antoine's. I was on my way to fulfilling my dream with plenty of cash and a growing reputation as a Chef de Cuisine. Then the Pandemic came like a hurricane and annihilated humanity.

After the "calico incident," Fred's work in English and philosophy courses became obsessed. During his "tertulias" at his beautiful house on some Friday and Saturday evenings, I realized Fred was a depressed man from the poems and papers he read. The house was built by Fred's great-grandfather and had the aroma of antiquity. It was a country home when it was constructed. The mansion was a registered historical site. Unfortunately, during the depression, when the family's other businesses were imperiled and there was a need for liquidity, most of the land was sold in large parcels. The houses had to follow the antebellum-style to ensure an upper-class neighborhood. The result was two blocks of green with a gigantic antebellum home surrounded by trees and myriad antebellum-style houses of a smaller, block-size, still palatial, surrounding it. I found a description of an antebellum house as a building planned to be on a grand scale with an overall blocky form. The symmetrical facade features large, evenly spaced windows and stately Greek-style columns or pillars. Porticos with triangular front pediments shelter both the front and rear entrances. Spacious balconies and covered porches encircle nearly the entire exterior. The roof is typically hipped or gabled and crowned with a roomy central Italianate cupola, or onion dome, that formerly offered a view of the plantation grounds. The interior is also designed with sumptuousness: features include enormous foyers, sweeping open stairways, ballrooms, grand dining rooms, and intricate design work. The design work included complex shapes and patterns made from plaster to adorn walls and furniture. It was also used to create wood and floor designs.

About six or seven of us would meet in the library (the beauty and the number of books and other paraphernalia was humbling) at Fred's house and spend the weekend smoking weed and reading. Discussion groups reviewed a relevant author, our own poetry readings, and many other events that combined studying and smoking cannabis and experimenting with mushrooms. We went there about two weekends per month. During the fall and spring, when the temperature lowered and a cool breeze was in the air, Fred's parents would come and spend a few days in Baton Rouge. Two servants took care of the mansion twenty-four hours, except they would disappear to their quarters when Fred was staying. During the week, Fred stayed at a fraternity house, Phi Beta Chi, where his father and great-grandfathers had been members while studying at Harvard. Coincidentally, LSU had a chapter, so Fred was received by the fraternity with open arms. Fred took me to the tertulia the first time I visited his mansion because I did not have a car. The other students in the group had cars and were progenies to wealthy families. I had the advantage of having expended all the time at home reading most of the authors we were discussing. Unlike many teenagers, I spent the time I had available for socializing in the New Orleans Public Library. I needed to understand these writers better the first time I read them. The terms "fear and trembling," "bad faith," and "authenticity" became jargon for us.

I am still determining how many years have passed since the pandemic advent and how many people are left in the Quarter and whether all animals have disappeared. The mesmerizing drizzle lingers and generates wrangling feelings within me. Should I end it all as so many have done already? There was a broadcast at noon every day informing how progress was being made. That patience was imperative to win the war against the virus. No one knew its origins, and disinformation with a myriad of sinister theories as to the origins of the virus grew like a weed on shortwave and other platforms. All platforms ceased broadcasting, people in the Quarter began to disappear, and I felt alone and lonely. I want to maintain the objective of these pages, which is not to write my own confessions. I liked the world to know about this authentic individual. Nevertheless, since the world as we know it does not exist, I should give an account of my last years in it.

A cold wind was sieving the refined rain that fell on me as I walked out of the Saint Ann Building and strolled down Bourbon towards Canal. The Quarter was deserted, and I feared most people were dead. I must admit there are some very personal revelations on these pages. If I knew someone would read them, I would hesitate to write these confessions. My defective sexual organ precipitated my discovery of other means to engage people sexually. Thus, I became a cunning linguist. I practiced fellatio on those well-connected individuals who came to the restaurants where I worked all those years and solicited me—only prominent men. I disliked the practice, but it allowed me entry into many vital places. Cunnilingus, however, was my favorite, and many women in New Orleans enjoyed my tongue a great deal.

It all started when I was fifteen and was working as a busboy at "The Court of Two Sisters." A significant politician in New Orleans's government took me to a secluded room upstairs and made me fellate him. There were rooms for two upstairs where assignations frequently took place. The pairs were usually a married man meeting his lover or a gay man in the closet meeting with a paramour. This happened to me about four times during that first summer of work. They tried to give me cash in payment, and I refused. However, my salary as a busboy changed from .55 cents an hour, in addition to the tips the waiters cared to share, to $2.00. I was told the management was pleased with my work and hoped that I continue busing for them during the summer. The scholarship I had at Jesuit grew financially so that my books, uniforms, school trips, and many other benefits were automatically paid in addition to tuition. It appears that one of the men I had fellated was a devoted catholic and a Jesuit High benefactor. The following summer, I refused any invitation unless it was from someone important. I did not care to consume the semen I was forced to ingest since they held my head steady as they came into my mouth.

One evening the following summer, as we closed the restaurant, I found a tipsy lesbian crying copiously. I asked how I could help. At which point she answered, "eat me." That expression I knew was one of dismissal, and I started turning to the door when she said: "Lock the door." I locked the door, turned around, and found that she had lowered her magnificent designer pants and was sitting at the edge of the table with her beautiful manicured yoni half open, showing her engorged lips the color of passion fruit. Indeed, it was God's gift to man. Since I was tall, I kneeled on a pillow and began devouring her; after a minute, I found myself transported to gourmet heaven where a salty, saline sauce gratifyingly overwhelmed my taste buds. My olfactory receptors were having an orgy. At seventeen, I had found my calling. She cried with pleasure, and I realized we were not alone in the building as someone was trying to open the door. She pulled up her pants as I cleansed my mouth with one of the Court of Two Sisters' beautiful linen napkins and rushed to the door. As I opened the door, she cried at the back of the room, talking loudly about a loved one's death. The waiter who was trying to open the door asked what had happened. Mabel Amelia (I had recognized the influential real estate magnate) told him she did not feel well and could she borrow the busboy for a minute to take her to the taxi stand. She held on to my arm and went downstairs to look for a taxi; and at the same time gave me a phone number to call her and do the same again.

I called her, wanting to see her again, and she asked me where I lived. I told her that I was staying at a Rooming House on Esplanade. She told me she had a better place for me and that I should expect an envelope from the Court. The envelope was waiting for me the next day and contained a lease. Mabel Amelia became my mentor/benefactor in so many ways. She found me a place in St. Ann and provided me with clients, funds, and relevant books such as the one published by Lujon Press, *The Anatomy of the Clitoris for Linguists*. I suspect it was a vanity publication with very few copies printed. I did not find anything like the book she gave me in the many university libraries I had visited after the pandemic. I had glorious library moments at Tulane, Loyola, UNO, and many other universities in the area, and I borrowed quite a collection of books on the subject that are in my apartment.

Until I met Mabel, neither women nor men appealed to me sexually. After my first sexual experience with her, new erotic horizons appeared before me. I felt something around my defective penis and an incredible sensation through my olfactory nerves and taste buds—sublime! The vaginal secretions, combined with transudate, gave the aroused pussy a sea-salt taste and aroma. This scent gave me the idea to prepare sauces and dishes that would go well with the Caribbean beach aroma. These depended on the client or the pussy; I would have the right condiments, the correct sauce, and what have you to formulate a marvelous experience. The number of fairy godmothers recommended by Mabel grew to fifteen when I was a freshman at LSU. I would return to New Orleans on the weekends we did not have tertulias, and some of my fairy godmothers would see me then. At first, only Mabel had a key to my apartment, and by the time I was in Baton Rouge, most of the fairies had keys. It was a fascinating experience since I never knew what I would find in my apartment when I was back. The fairies remodeled everything: a large circular bed, satin sheets, a well-stocked kitchen, a myriad of books, envelopes with cash, and bookcases are a few examples.

In addition to giving me the book, Mabel tutored me, or rather my tongue, how to navigate the labia majora and labia minora and reach under the clitoral hood until the female screams with ecstasy. I also had an advantage over most people: my tongue was longer than usual: it could almost reach the g-spot in some women. This gave them an added measure of pleasure. I also used an insertable vibrator while caressing the pussy with my tongue and lips—lips to lips. It was also noteworthy the different types of orgasms the fairies had: The most interesting one was the "squirter." This type of female ejaculation fascinated me from the first moment I witnessed it while steering my tongue under and around the clitoral hood. Although I have read in one of the myriads of books that have become my property after visits to libraries, the so-called squirt is more of a predictor that an orgasm is approaching. The first time it occurred, it was quite a surprise. I was under the impression she was urinating as the squirt stroked my cheek. The most dramatic orgasm, however, triggered a panic attack. The woman fainted, and I was not sure if she was deceased. I waited for two minutes, and she was unconscious with no signs of being alive. I called Mabel immediately, and she explained that it was typical for her to faint after the climax. I did not know any of their names, and they apparently knew each other well. The fairies came from different sexual tastes: lesbians, bisexuals, and heteros. They were in their sixties, and it was evident they took good care of their bodies. I never had personal conversations with them: we dedicated our entire time to discussing sex and performing it. They had their particular ways of having intercourse and I accommodated them.

I am happy to say that they allowed me most of the time to practice my culinary experiments in which their pussy was one of the most important ingredients. For me eating/devouring pussy was a statement of fact. I marinated the yoni with different sauces that together with the pussy juices blended into an exquisite elixir.

I prepared a French dressing for the female who fainted to coat her labia majora, labia minora, and the frenulum of the labia--including the clitoris and its prepuce. I used a very fine painter's brush that I would submerge a couple of times in the half cup of the brew before coating the pussy. These are the ingredients: Onion juice, cider vinegar, celery seed, and the salt would be provided by the yoni's juices. I would brush gently noticing the degree of arousal before beginning to suckle like a hungry child.

Unfortunately, the first pussy meals I had were too many in a short period of time and my lingual frenulum suffered as a result. The frenulum is a soft tissue mucosa which extends from the ventral surface of the tongue, in the midline, to the floor of the mouth. The part attached to the floor of the mouth was detaching and bleeding a few drops. Such an incident brought about my having to carry a calendar book on my pocket. I started to limit the number of fairies I would eat per week. By the time I was chef at Antoine's, their number had dwindled to three or four. Some died, others no longer had the longing. Those were some wonderful years particularly the ones when some of the fairies wanted to talk about themselves rather than be devoured. There are quite a few stories I have yet to tell. My fairies were so unlike the ones I had read in fairy tales and yet they provided me with a joyous life.

By this time, I had decided to leave LSU since I had reached the level of "Chef de Partie" and several restaurants were offering me a higher position in their kitchens. My interest in English originated from my doing a great deal of reading at Jesuit and my wanting to learn to write poetry. Such was no longer the case. I wanted to end my days as a Chef in a five-star restaurant in Paris. I decided to leave LSU with some syllabi of courses that look interesting and do the reading on my own. It worked out very well until the Pandemic came and carried all my dreams with it.

Outside the drizzle continues. This is a very interesting way to end the world—with a quiet whimper. I always thought, and it was discussed during some tertulias, that there would be an atomic incident/accident that would wreck the world. I remember discussing the film "On the Beach," as a realistic ending of the world. What is happening now is contrary to what most humans expected. I have travelled a great deal throughout the southern states without encountering humans. I found traces of surviving humans without actually seeing any. I decided that the plan of action would be to visit the wealthiest areas of very large southern cities and see what I can find in the houses. I am very disappointed in the results I am getting. I found some generators and a large amount of canned food, but nothing out of the ordinary. I keep hoping to find paintings by established masters: Picasso and Warhol. At first, I felt it was bizarre to enter those houses and stumble on humans and animals' corpses, which now were mostly mounds of unknown composition. Now

I am used to the mounds of ashes, small and/or large, depending on age and size. Nevertheless, I keep hoping to find other human beings.

Fred, I gather from his journals, stories and the tertulias, fell madly in love with a fifteen-year-old Vietnamese female who worked at the Mogolla's house on Esplanade Avenue. Her moniker "Tay" (hands) was very fitting because after five minutes of receiving her massage your fantasy of having intercourse with her would disappear. Her hands were the typical small hands of a fifteen-year-old Vietnamese female. They were soft and very strong. She wore a white uniform which differentiate her from the other girls in the place. Mogolla has purchased her from a Vietnamese coyote the year before. Mogolla's two story mansion was held prisoner on the middle of a very large lot with a cement wall crowned with iron spikes and a large number of trees that concealed the house. One entered through the driveway which opened its wide doors as a car approached and a uniformed man would approach the car and identify the passengers and open the large iron doors and they would drive a short distance to the front of the house behind the trees. This was a private club with a restricted number of members. Only a limited number of guests were allowed per night and the members were required to make an appointment a week in advance. The group of selected members, who were mostly from the carnival parade or krewes (Rex and Comus), could invite up to one guest to the Club Mogolla. It was whispered that the Madam was a lover of one of the distinguished members.

A large porch going around the first floor with giant white faux Corinthian columns greeted you. The second floor had a wrap-around balcony where one would see some of the guests engaged in private conversations. The place was used for political meetings, business exchanges, and many other issues that required a private place. As one entered the front door, there would be a foyer that had to the left a small room to leave overcoats, umbrellas, etc., and to the right a very large room with sliding doors that opened to the bar and private booths. There were other rooms downstairs I did not visit. The second floor was reached by taking a wide set of stairs that led to where several different types of private rooms were located. There were two rooms for massages. The other rooms had different names and referred to the type of sex allowed to take place: Anilingus/Klimasphilia, Japanese Bondage, Blindfold/Asphyxiation, Urophilia, Zentai, and others. Each girl had a specialty which was displayed in private. Fred took me to the place twice and the visit and his writings gave me a very good idea of the place origins.

I suppose Fred probably wanted to know if I was gay. I only wanted a massage, I told him, and "Hands" gave me an unforgettable massage. However, I kept my shorts on so that she was not able to see my genitals—I suspect Fred was very disappointed when she told him.

Tay was brought to New Orleans by child traffickers and Mogolla--who did business with them--purchased the fifteen-year-old Vietnamese girl. Fred, who became obsess with the girl, offered the Madam twice the amount she had paid for the child and she refused. Whereupon Fred spoke to her lover, a very important man in city politics, a member of Comus, and the girl was Fred's property thereafter. The building on Saint Ann had a Mansard roof where two apartments were rented by the week to tourists, and other individuals interested in short stays without having to go to a hotel. Fairy Godmother managed to get me the one facing west and Hands was given the apartment across from mine, facing east. Such position gave me a good perspective of Hands and Fred. He hired several retired teachers to tutor her in English, History, Math, and other subjects to prepare her to enter 10th grade at the prestigious Academy of the Sacred Heart on Saint Charles. I am certain his influential friends help him to have her accepted in one of the best women schools in New Orleans. I remembered seeing her wearing her uniform and I then understood Fred's temptation. A car with a driver would be in front of the building every weekday morning to take her to school. She graduated with good grades, as expected, since she had a high IQ. All this information I obtained from Fred's journals who wrote just about everything in his life with due diligence. After High School she began her studies at Loyola University with the goal of becoming a school teacher. She again had a driver that would take her to the University those days in which she had classes. Fred's dreams became a nightmare when, after a year studying at Loyola, Hands disappeared. She left all her possessions in the apartment—even her toothbrush. Such an event depressed Fred and, to some extent changed Fred.

Every morning and afternoon, I scanned all frequencies in my battery-operated radio, hoping I would hear human voices. This morning there was a recording calling for all survivors to go to the CDC in Atlanta. As I walked out of my apartment a cold breeze was piercing the drops of rain in the deserted streets of the Quarter. The drops fell on the street producing a syncopated sound that reverberated in the silence of the surroundings. I was using a motorcycle I had liberated from the police station located in the Quarter. Motor bikes navigated easily through the thousands of abandoned cars in the highways and the police motorcycles had very large saddlebags that allowed me to carry a great deal. I found as well a raincoat that became very handy since it is raining everywhere. Raining is not the correct word it is more like drizzling since that streets are wet but never to the point of flooding. It appears that with the Pandemic came climate change. I had driven to Baton Rouge and Biloxi when I first ventured out of the Quarter some ten years ago (I no longer know how long it has been since the Pandemic appeared). Those trips showed me that driving a car was impractical: the myriad of accidents in the highways that blocked the lanes, not to mention the fires. The fires were everywhere: large areas were now cinders and explosions from gas leaks were common. Columns of dark smoke soaring everywhere one look. I took along a syphon pump to make easier to get gasoline from all those abandoned vehicles. The cities reminded me of the ruins in the news clips I had seeing of WWII. The skeletons of large buildings, and the remains of houses where families once lived, were prominently displayed along the way. The odor of decaying violets was ubiquitously.

When I arrived in Atlanta, I went directly to the CDC building, but it was closed. I knocked on all the doors, threw rocks at the windows, and broke several to no avail—no one was around. I waited in the parking area for a few days and no humans appeared. Actually, nothing emerged—not even pigeons. I cruised around Atlanta for a few days, inspected a handful of mansions, went to a few stores, and no humans were about. I brought back to the Quarter a few things, and concluded I was the only human left in the world.

I continued reading Fred's journals and the following passage from *Steppenwolf* is relevant "[...] I wish to leave my own personality as far as possible in the background. I do not want to put down my own confessions, to tell a story or to write an essay on psychology, but simply as an eye witness to contribute something to the picture of this peculiar individual [...]. Further on Hesse writes that "Solitude is independence." I concurred with him since I had attained it all those years before the Pandemic stroke, but now I am not so sure--not after this savage and dismal catastrophe of nature. I am curious to see how much a human can endure. In some cases, exemplified by some of the Quarter residents, not much and they killed themselves. I wonder how much I can bear before I blow my brains. I am always hoping for the best so I will be here until I die from old age. I must admit that despair frequently overwhelms me. It is a sickness of the spirit. Can one say that all is lost to me as a result? No. I move on looking for other humans. I am stunned by the irony, by the way in which the gods amuse themselves. Here I am, a man who was rejected by his birth parents, survived childhood by working his way through life, and somehow managed to endure this epidemic. Whereas, privileged humans such as Fred, did not. Granted Fred was killed by a jealous husband before the outbreak of the blight. The pandemic is another example of the gods killing us for sport. I do not believe what I read somewhere that a man should be proud of suffering: because all suffering is a reminder of our high state. According to Nietzsche, many died too late, and a few die too early. No one died at the right time during this pandemic: I wonder what Zarathustra would say about it. Fred had been full of pride, always the cleverest, always the most eager, always one step ahead of the others, always the scholar and the intellectual. Perhaps all his seeking prevented him from finding his goal.

I exist because I think, and I cannot stop myself from thinking. Like Sartre, along with the thinking nausea appears and begins to entice me unto death. However, nothingness is baser than nausea.

After reading Fred's stories and journals I determined that for him the meaning of life, the reason for existing became sex. He trolled the streets and bars in the Quarter looking for women. Such behavior resulted in his death. I found an unfinished story entitled "Searching for a Story," which describes his pursuit of women tourists in the Quarter. His characters had different names and sometimes he used his own:

> "Jesse, during those nights when inspiration escaped him, he decided he had to write; he felt deep inside, there was a story to compose, and it was kicking inside him trying to escape. "I am pregnant," he would say to himself, and then smoke

a joint in his apartment at the corner of Saint Ann and Bourbon, and begin his usual path...Leaves his apartment and turns right, away from Bourbon Street and the Mississippi, and when he gets to Dauphine turns left and leisurely walks toward Canal Street, traversing Orleans, St. Peter, Tolouse, St. Louis, Conti, Bienville, Iberville and stops at a location that is now a hotel built at the site that the New Orleans Opera occupied. He knows the black doormen at the hotel so he jives with them for a while, determining if there are any lone tourist females staying at the hotel. He would usually give them a tip to make sure they would keep him informed. If there is nothing available, he continues his stroll on Iberville in the direction of the river. There he would check "La casa de los Marinos," and on to Saint Peter and stopped at "The Seven Seas" a hang-out for quarterites. He believed most of the females there were walking STD's. One evening, he was informed that a group of females had arrived from northern Louisiana and were ready to party. He waited around until the doorman pointed to a female who was looking at the display outside the hotel that advertised play by local amateur actors. He approached and started a conversation which led to a drink in "La Casa," later in "The Seas," and then on to his place where they would have some weed and sex.

The above was one of the sketches he had written which later he would adorn with descriptive residue and descriptions of the female: how she looked, and their naked encounter. He would talk a great deal about the appearance of the bars and people in them. In this instance, it appears that the woman was being abused by her husband for one reason in particular—she could not have children. Fred gave her information about a shelter in New Orleans that took care of abused women. My hypothesis is that one of these husbands killed Fred when the wife confessed her infidelity.

Another sketch, which was not signed, deals with an older man who was one of the oldest residents in the apartments, and who was killed by street people. I am not certain of the authorship. It is possible that Fred's maternal uncle was the author. "Mr. Eldridge" portrays a retired old man who worked for many years for the New Orleans Public Service and lived in an apartment below where I live now, on the second floor. I found newspaper clippings and photos that gave details about the incident. Mr. Eldridge would go around the Quarter during the coldest winter nights looking for homeless people sleeping on doorways and in the streets and gave them shelter in the building on Saint Ann. At first these homeless were camping in the foyer which caused quite a commotion among the residents. As a result, he decided to allow them to stay in his apartment. Such move resulted in his demise. The newspaper articles gave a sketch of his life and his work for NOPS. I suspect that because of the coverage his life received in the papers, Fred or his uncle decided that a story about him was not significant.

The next story is also unsigned and unfinished. It appears to be of a junky overdosed in one of the apartments.

"The junk merchant doesn't sell his product to the consumer, he sells the consumer to his product. He does not improve and simplify his merchandise. He degrades and simplifies the client."

William S. Burroughs

JUNKY

Leonard Bergé was a junky. He resided in a luxurious apartment in Saint Ann Street in the Quarter. The apartment where his parents had relegated him was on the corner of Bourbon Street and Saint Ann. His use of the needle was a process of several years from when he was a senior at Warren Easton High School until he dropped from L.S.U., some three years later. His family was very well off thanks to the patriarch who had done extremely well with his cotton fields in Mississippi. Everyone had heard his grandfather's name in Southeastern Mississippi: Patrice Atkins. He had negotiated some sweetheart deals that had provided him with an extraordinary inheritance for his grandchildren. Leo had been expected to go to an Ivy League school and become a banker in New York. Unfortunately, he became prey to speedballs, and his parents had insulated him from family and friends to prevent unpleasant circumstances. In the last four years, his appearance had changed from that of a muscular young man to a decrepit old man. His naked figure would bring to mind the photographs of Indian mystics. His ribs would show like bars on a cage covered with some pale membrane. His thin limbs hung at his side like cables surging out of an electric outlet, swaying like windmills impelled by the breeze. His head bent down, always staring at the ground as if he were looking for a lost object. It gave his body the shape of a hook.

His first experience with smack was accidental. After doing an enormous amount of grass, he felt it was time to experience a more intense experience. The contraption handed to him to inject horse was totally unfamiliar and he didn't know how to use. The person, the "sugar man," perhaps, who was the host of a very selective gathering, was kind enough to inject him with junk for the first time. The man took his arm and examined very meticulously with long, cold, crafty fingers, looking for a vessel. He then, with a junky smile commented that Leo had the ideal junky arms, covered with rivers of blood vessels. The speedball went into his circulatory system and began to spit firecrackers that exploded silently and catapulted him into a nihilist universe. Leo's body began to melt until it metamorphosed into a blob of protoplasm that flowed along every crevice and contour of the wall against which his back leaned and the pillow upon which he sat. The protoplasm began to slide slowly, very slowly, down from where his back rested to the floor like butter dripping from a hot knife. He found himself lying on the floor and a light in the ceiling slapping his face, tearing his eyes from the painful experience. His head began to spin as if it had been placed in a washing machine. That first experienced hooked him and there was nothing else he wanted out life. His downward spiral began that day and he no longer care about family or friends. The only person who visited him was his pusher when Leo needed to replenish his stash.

It is evident that the story is inspired by William S. Burroughs *Naked Lunch*. Unfortunately, it is not finished and I will never know what the end was going to be. I suspect Leo was going to die from an overdose after giving information about his very short and unhappy life.

The following story was published in a collection of stories under a pseudonym. The title of the collection of short stories is *Gothic Stories*. I found some of those stories in their original manuscript which appears to be different to the final publication. The following story is based on crime executed by a troubled young man. Fred or his uncle used the crime as a basis for the story with much descriptive residue and the epistolary method. It should be noted that the calico cat incident appears as motif in several stories.

Board of Pardons
Louisiana Parole Board
P.O. Box 94304
Baton Rouge, Louisiana 70804

TO WHOM IT MAY CONCERN

I have been asked by my attorneys to write a letter on my behalf for the forthcoming hearing on my possible parole after serving thirty-seven years for killing a young woman, Ashley Robichaux, in New Orleans. I hope that the following narration will shed some light on my heinous behavior.

Several decades have passed since the tragic events I am about to narrate occurred, and yet, the incidents are still as vivid as if I had experienced them yesterday. But, in fact, they are like a dying sun swallowed by murky clouds. I was nineteen and had recently undergone the trauma of losing both of my parents in a plane crash. The cause, according to investigators, was wind shear. As the plane was taking off from the New Orleans International Airport one rainy morning, it crashed in the bayous surrounding the airport. The irony was that it had been a chartered plane to Las Vegas where my parents were going for the weekend. My father worshiped the Roman goddess Fortuna, the patron of gamblers, who failed him in this instance. There were no survivors. My father was a prominent attorney in the "Crescent City" and my mother was a professor of Comparative Literature at Tulane. They had great expectations for me. Either as an attorney joining my father's firm, or becoming a professor at Tulane. I had failed to do well in the S.A.T. so that the only option I had was to attend Tulane as an English mayor thanks to my mother's position. I was not interested in higher education, so I attended the University to please my parents. After their death, I continue to attend part time out of respect for their memory. I loved to read and I was writing poetry, so that attending classes, and taking only the courses I cared for without expecting a degree, was my life for the moment. I considered myself an existential hero searching for a story. Hesse's novel, *Steppenwolf,* had become my favorite reading. The pronunciation of the German title *Steppenvolf* sounded like music to my ears. But truth was that I was devastated. The death of my parents had driven me close to insanity. I rambled in a fog of sterile, toneless, and flat existence. I was frequently contemplating suicide and how to carry it out. I walked in the shadows between rationality and insanity like a soldier warily stepping on a mined field. There were several possibilities: jumping into the Mississippi, using my father's gun, an overdose of sleeping pills, and many other possibilities depending on how dark the day was. During my most dismal moments I would put my father's vintage Luger in my mouth while submerging myself in self-pity, envisioning the trajectory of the projectile and a crater erupting on the top of my head spewing blood and bones and brains. Dad was a WWII veteran and had removed the gun from the body of a German officer who had committed suicide discharging it in his mouth. Father had joined the Army at seventeen at the tail end of the War and participated in the mopping-up of Berlin. According to him, there was a machine gun nest on the second floor of a building that had his squad immobilized. He managed to climb very close to it, so as to throw a grenade that killed three German soldiers, and with the adrenalin flowing through his veins to the point he felt he could fly and do just about anything, he killed an additional one with his rifle as he went into the room while at the same time receiving a light wound on his upper arm. As he went into the room, a Captain in the German army was putting the gun into his mouth and firing. My father was decorated with a Silver Star for gallantry in action and received a Purple Heart for the wound. Father loved to narrate the anecdote and indulged in the details of the crater on the top of the head and the blood and bones covering it. I could taste the metal and the oil of the barrel for my father had spent many hours cleaning and oiling it after his forays into the swamps shooting at everything that moved. The barrel of the gun was like a pacifier evoking the early years in my life when sucking a rubber nipple lured me to sleep during those solitary nights when my parents went away on their long trips and I was left alone with my black nanny. My only companion then was a calico cat that spent most of her time in my bedroom, sleeping at my feet. Evidently my psyche was too fragile to stand the loss of loved ones. I was ten years old the first time I became aware of my flaw—if one can labeled as such. My calico cat, Calita, at the age of eight, was found dead in our back yard. It was the first time I confronted the death of a loved one. For several months I sailed into a severe depression which resulted in my spending over a year with an analyst. I was under Dr. Thompson's care until I was finally able to forget about Calita and her presence in my bedroom from the time I was two. Since I did not want to begin visiting a psychiatrist again, I managed to find three physicians who provided me with a substantial amount of bennies and downers to keep me up when I so desired, and be able to sleep when I got tired. I was also able to find a steady supplier of Marihuana to add to my chemical defenses against depression and suicide. I lived in a fog for most of those years and my recollection of her is the only vivid memory of that period.

Thanks to my medical history of psychological trauma and the help of my father's firm, I was able to obtain an "I F" classification for military service and thus, avoided the Viet Nam War. While many friends and acquaintances that graduated or dropped out of college were drafted, I was able to maintain a life of leisure without concerning myself with a war far away.

I sold my parent's house in the Garden District and bought a townhouse on Saint Phillip, in the French Quarter. I had inherited a total of four million dollars from my parents between the life insurance, the partnership in the Law Firm had some assets for survivors, several investments from my father, real state property in Kenner, all of those assets were liquidated and I put the money on a combination of bonds, as suggested by the Law Firm's accountant. I was a man of leisure, as a result of the monthly income these investments provided so I was marching through life without having to work, without financial concerns, and yet I was as unhappy as a drunk living on skid road.

Since literature was so easy for me—perhaps my mother's influence and genes—I had been concentrating on it and ignoring the usual requirements for a degree. Mother had had a great influence on my love for literature. From the time I can remember, there was I in her arms, nursing from her breast as she read from a book. She also wrote a great deal, publishing largely literary criticism in many journals and books published in some prestigious university presses. During the time of her untimely demise, my poor mother had been recording her experiences in her memoirs. Her life had been extraordinary and eventful: escaping the Holocaust, night rides, hiding in ruins and under bridges, all those things were now lost: unleaving weeping willow leaves crushed by a storm and her tears were evaporated in a rain of fire. I cherished the moments before going to bed when she described to me the horrors she witnessed and the perils she went through. She took a thick notebook with a leather cover everywhere for her Germanic upbringing prodded her to write all those memories that were like snapshots in her mind every available moment. Her remembrances will not be shared with anyone since the manuscript was burned in the crash.

I was named after my father and grandfather. Actually, I was the fourth in the line of Claude Courbet which extended, as far as I know, to the middle of the Nineteenth century to my great grandfather who was a river boat captain in the Mississippi river. I told my friends and acquaintances that my name was Harry, since I really did not care for my first name. Mother gave me her father's name, Heinrich, as my middle name.

I had enough courses to be a senior in literature, notwithstanding the fact that I was only a junior on overall credits. Because of my good grades and because of family history, I was able to convince the Chair of the English Department to allow me to take two graduate seminars. One was on Twentieth Century British Poets, which met Mondays 5:00-8:00 p.m. and a seminar on James Joyce, which met Wednesdays 5:00-8:00 p.m. I met Ashley in the James Joyce seminar, although in my journals and dreams she was Hermina. She was a doctoral student finishing her course work. As a result of this schedule, I would go home after classes, and change into some old jeans and a t-shirt and some old Mexican sandals with soles made from automobile tires. After a frugal meal and some reading, I would arrive at the **Seven Seas** around eleven, after ingesting a couple of bennies and smoking a joint. I carried with me a mochila where I kept the pistol, a small note book where I wrote poetry and any impressions worth writing and/or remembering, wallet and a couple of bennies, in case I came down before the usual time. The **Seas** was located on Saint Phillip about two blocks from my house. I did not have a car and my trip to Tulane on class days took 40-45 minutes by street car each way. It was extremely difficult to find a place to park in the Quarter so I had sold the three cars we had and I did not miss my Mustang. When one lives in the Quarter one tends to remain in the place without going too far out of it. The Quarter becomes a microcosm where there is a suspension of the ethical and the typical mores and the commonplace laws are discontinued in favor of a bohemian life that allows a freedom that one does not find elsewhere. To live in the Quarter was to dwell in a perpetual moral holiday where time was obliterated and all the days were Saturdays. The **Seven Seas** was a bar frequented by the locals after 11:00 p.m. Before eleven, it was usually filled with tourists and young kids. During these years the drinking age in New Orleans was eighteen and the **Seas** filled with teeny-boppers whose parents expected them by midnight. The bar had been once upon a time a large eighteenth century residence that had had its walls plucked and was now one large single room that extended North to South. It was 50 feet from North to South and 30 feet from East to West. At the western part of the room was a large bar with stools that extended three fourths of the room and had a wall mirror with shelves that held a myriad of bottles of liquor. The entrance to the bar was located at the southern part on the side of the bar so that all the newcomers passed by the bar first and then moved on to the eastern part of the room where all the tables and booths were. The only light in this area was provided by three pseudo-Tiffany lamps that hung over three chess tables where many customers played practically twenty-four hours a day since the bar never closed. Inasmuch as the bar had only two small fluorescent lights close to the ceiling where the mirror ended, the entire room was in a perpetual state of duskiness except in the early morning when the janitors cleaned the floors and bathrooms of the vomit, papers, gum, rubbers, needles, cigarette butts and drugs left by the customers. Leaning against and midway of the eastern wall was a jukebox that was endlessly playing popular songs. I frequently fed it quarters and played "I can't keep my eyes off of you" the Frankie Vallie hit of the previous year. I would then look at her from my throne, her beautiful face now faded by time like a photograph exposed to the sun, and smile whenever her steely blue eyes strayed my way, and I whispered along with the song "I love you baby..."

On the North west side of the room was a corridor that led to the restrooms and the patio, where those who did not know any better tried to smoke weed and were frequently busted by the narcs that frequented the place. On the edge of the corridor was a broken, old ping-ball machine that I used as a perch. Since I knew the owner, I was the only person allowed to sit on the tall side of the machine from where I had a wonderful vista of the entire room and, for the most part, the shadows of the people in it. Most importantly, I could see her face always sitting at the same place in the southwest part of the bar. Whenever I played the song, sometimes our eyes will meet as the juke box played "you are too good to be true," and sometimes she would smile back, a Mona Lisa type of smile where the eyes, her clear blue eyes, her sparkling blue eyes that reflected the neon signs framing and peppering the large rectangular mirror of the bar, were doing the smiling. "I wanna hold you so much." Weeks and then months passed before I finally developed the courage to speak to her. Although we were in the same seminar, there was very little interaction between the two of us. Until the night she was leaving rather late and she seemed unable to walk straight, I offered to walk her home. I took her to an apartment she had two blocks beyond where mine was and, to my surprise, after inviting me to prepare myself and her some coffee, she returned from the bathroom totally nude. I must explain at this point the fact that I have difficulty interacting with women. The only woman I had known carnally at this point was a prostitute. When I was fourteen, my father felt I was too close to my mother and that my behavior was feminized, and, therefore, he felt it was his duty to make sure I did not become a homosexual. He took me to a very private and exclusive Bordello in Jefferson Parish where a young woman introduced me to sex. I was extremely embarrassed about the entire episode to the point where I had kept myself from having sex since then. As a result of my ignorance, the experience with Hermina was a disaster. I ejaculated prematurely and she was very annoyed. But she was heaven to the touch! As my fingers moved about her body, her alabaster skin, her red hair, a Pre-Raphaelite model, her erect red nipples gorged with blood, were very arousing and my self-control failed me that day. Thereafter she did not speak to me and she never looked in my direction at the Seas. I was devastated, even though she was almost a decade older, I was ready to marry her. I wrote to her proposing matrimony; I told her how much money I had, but she did not reply to my letters and then one night, at the Seas, a gorilla warned me to stay away from her if I wanted to stay healthy. At this point my stalking of Hermina began. I contacted the make-up artist of the Pretenders Little Theater on Dumaine and Saint Ann who sold me several wigs and showed me how to change my appearance without ever asking me compromising questions. Using a myriad of costumes, I followed her practically everywhere she went in the Quarter. Until one evening, as

I watched across the street from her apartment, I saw her kissing another woman. They stopped kissing and looked in my direction and started to laugh. A cloud entered my brain and I only remember taking the gun from the bag, crossing the street and shooting both of them. I inserted the gun in my mouth and pulled the trigger but it jammed. Suddenly, I felt a blow on my face and I fainted. When I woke up I was handcuffed in a police car. The trial was swift and thanks to my age and my state of mind, the judge was merciful enough and did not sentence me to death. I hereby throw myself to the mercy of the Board and request I be paroled.

Thank you very much for your kind attention to this matter. I look forward to hearing from you.

Very truly yours, Claude H Courbet

The next story, VIETVET, seems to have several narrators and is based on a terrorist who bombed two buildings in New Orleans.

VIETVET

Randy Fontenot was a proud Coonass from Eunice, Louisiana. [*Coonass, or Coon-ass, is a term for a person of Cajun ethnicity. Some view it as derogatory. However, many Cajun embrace the name. The term is believed to originate from the French word "conasse," meaning a fool.* Wikipedia] He, unfortunately, came from a family of losers, starting with his father, who died from a drug overdose when Randy was ten. He had three elder siblings: two boys and a girl. The boys had dropped out of high school and were laborers wherever they could find work. They seemed to be following their father's footsteps doing much drinking and drugs. Randy's sister had fallen very low on the ethical, moral, and legal scale: giving birth to three children from three different fathers. Her children were taken away by social services because of her addiction to smack and other drugs. She was very slim, and her cheekbones seemed to want to pierce her cheeks and run away. She had no teeth left, which explained why the skin of her cheeks seemed to be touching each other. I will let Harriet Beecher Stowe describe her: "[. . .] a miserable haggard woman, with large, wild eyes, sunken cheeks, disheveled matted hair, and long, lean hands, like a bird's claws [. . .]." These three siblings had left home, and

Randy was left to live with his mother, who worked at a grocery store and gave him love, food, and shelter. While in school, an English teacher named Sophia decided that the young Randy was talented and should attend college. Randy's American College Test (ACT) scores proved her correct in her boy assessment. Sophia went as far as to search for scholarships and found him a tuition scholarship for LSUBR.

Considering his family background, it was extraordinary that Randy was going to college. For the other expenses (dorm, meals, incidentals), Randy would work at one of the many restaurants in Tiger Town. He found a cheap rooming house a few blocks from the University. He worked full-time (sometimes more than ten hours) as a waiter and sometimes dishwasher on Tuesdays, Thursdays, and Saturdays. Mondays, Wednesdays, and Fridays, he had his classes. Sundays, he used to review the week's lectures and classes. He had decided to be an English teacher in Eunice, following in the footsteps of his English teacher. He managed school and work with difficulty but was on his way to obtaining a degree. Unfortunately, disaster struck when his mother had a heart attack and became disabled. This event obliged Randy to return to Eunice and care for his incapacitated mother. Randy assisted his mother, who did not recover from the heart attack and expired eight months later. There has been a misunderstanding about why the Draft Board grasped Randy so quickly. I will give more information on that point soon.

Those eight months were the most traumatic of Randy Fontenot's twenty-three-year life. Randy's mother was deeply indebted: the house had two or three mortgages, and her credit cards had been taken away by the banks—as a matter of speaking. In addition to the medical bills that kept coming like a serial nightmare. He had been working part-time since his mother required someone to be around 7/24. It would have been easy for someone with insurance to assist his mother because they would have provided a nurse for at least eight hours daily. When Randy went on his part-time job for about four hours per night, Ruby, his black neighbor, would take care of his mother for a small fee. He could keep all the bill collectors at bay until his mother's death, at which point most of that debt would be paid by different insurances. Randy, however, was very disturbed by the experience he had to deal with by himself. None of his siblings appeared, and some of his mother's brothers, nieces, and nephews came to visit once or twice. No one offered Randy help with the care of his mother, however. The continuous tension from bells he sometimes had to attend which indicated that medicine had to be given or that her blood pressure was rising. By the end of those last months of his mother's life, he was suicidal and decided to let the Viet Cong do it for him. The irony is that he was the only survivor of a squad of thirteen men. When he awoke in the hospital and received the news that he was the miracle man, he decided to cut the veins on his wrist. He was placed on a suicide watch and spent a long year in a Psychiatric Hospital. At this point, the omniscient narrator must intervene and give the readers some information about the draft as it existed during the war in Viet Nam. Most U.S. soldiers drafted during the Vietnam War were men from poor and working-class families. These young men would not obtain a college deferment, have a political connection, or have a family doctor that could give them a medical deferment. The SDS and Weather Underground asserted in some of their writings the Draft Board determined the selection of the draftees according to the following outline:

- High School Dropouts
- High School graduates not going to college
- College dropouts

In all these categories, blacks and Hispanics would be "preferred" over "white trash." Randy did not know the intricacies of the draft, so he failed to request the sole support of his mother's exemption. At the same time, she was ill and did not request a student deferment after she passed, and he was planning to return to LSU. [Some other texts claim Randy wanted to die and transferred his death to the hands of the Army.] His failure to contact the Draft Board resulted in him ending up in Viet Nam without knowing much about war and being poorly trained. He found himself in a squad of malcontents ambushed by the Vietcong and decimated. The squad of thirteen men had only one survivor, and Randy felt guilty about it for the rest of his life [Other documents suggest Randy was suicidal for other reasons]. His wounds were severe, and he was left with a limp because his right knee was crushed, and his chest was filled with scars from the number of shrapnel that struck him. He also had severe psychological issues that were revealed during his residence at the hospital. Ironically, his back would have a comparable experience years later, which I will explain briefly. Randy's guilt because he was the only survivor of his squad led to his being reminded in a behavioral health hospital. He attempted suicide several times, and bringing Randy back to reality would take time. [*Some of the previous information contradicted the Psychiatric Hospital, which indicates Randy joined the Army because he hoped the Viet Cong would kill him.*] While in the Psychiatric Hospital, Randy began to read/review some of the Marxist writers he had read and heard about during his two years at LSU. Randy felt that convalescing in the behavioral hospital was very fruitful because he read a great deal which gave him an advantage when he returned to classes. Furthermore, he now had the Army paying for all his college expenses, allowing him to attend political meetings and participate in other students' activities. Georg Lukacs, Marcuse, Sartre.

This biographical sketch, autobiography, fictionalized biography, short story, mini-story, tale—call it what you will—has many pencils and pen writings on the back and on the front of the page of the typewritten manuscript. Some additions and alternative realities are suggested on those accounts, and some contradict the information provided on those rumpled pages. His most-read authors appear to be Jean-Paul Sartre, Herbert Marcuse, Georg Lukács, and Antonio Gramsci. From their writings, he formulated a commitment that led to his becoming a Marxist and a member of SDS. Eventually, he joined the Weather Underground because he did not think SDS was militant enough for his views. Randy was fond of the detail that WU had taken the name from a Bob Dylan song: "You don't need a weatherman to know which way the wind blows." His indoctrination was expeditious since he read and felt that the deep state targeted him.

The meetings with the weathermen and his readings formulated a type of militancy that ends with death. Existentialism is the philosophical belief that we are each responsible for creating purpose, essence, or meaning in our lives. As we march through life, we accumulate that essence that determines our authenticity. We cease to be authentic whenever we act in bad faith concerning our values. Gods, governments, teachers, or other authorities do not give us our individual purpose and meaning.

For Marx, reification is not merely an illusion foisted upon consciousness from the outside but derives from the objective nature of social institutions; hence the critique of reified theories is never more than a preliminary to the analysis of the social relations which produce such reifications. Marcuse sees reification (also known as concretism, hypostatization, or the fallacy of misplaced concreteness) as a fallacy of ambiguity when an abstraction (abstract belief or hypothetical construct) is treated as if it were a concrete actual event or physical entity.

Randy reifies the Industrial, Corporatocracy, Military Complex as two (perhaps three—we will never know) buildings in New Orleans: The custom house where the draftees were given their physical and usually departed to book camp from that building. The other building was the Hibernia Bank on Carondelet. In addition, he was asking himself the question: "what, then, makes dying for cause self-sacrifice, as it usually seems to be? From Sartre, he borrowed the four words that perhaps describe his life: Isolation, Meaning, Freedom, and Death.

Randy first bombed the Customs House, which had quite an impact on the discussion of US involvement in Viet Nam. When he bombed the Hibernia building, he failed to calculate the time he needed to get away from the target safely and paid for it. His back was the recipient of a lot of detritus from the building's glass windows and wood and metal shards. He suffered an instantaneous death when his lungs and all the organs on the upper half of his body were impacted by the debris at such close proximity. The newspapers and the television stations had enough material to abuse and disinform the public for weeks.

The debate became on whether Randy was authentic. He took his commitment to the extreme in his battle with the Industrial, Corporatocracy, and Military Complex. Others classified him as a terrorist that had perished poetically and justly while committing a terrorist act. The text of these typewritten pages belongs to several authors: I suspect one of them knew Randy well enough to get into his unconsciousness. I do not believe the newspaper clippings I found with the typewritten manuscript could have provided enough information to delve into the young man's unconsciousness.

I have copied everything as it appears: on the typewritten manuscript and those portions are written in cursive. I am using for the first time an IBM Selectric Typewriter thanks to the collection of generators I have parked on the street. The Selectric makes typing much more leisurely and very pleasant. I went to the Universities looking for typewriters and, I am happy to report, it was a gold mine: the variety of typewriters is astonishing.

The next story I found is titled "Black Knight" and it tells the story of an illicit affair ending in tragedy. I believe Fred wrote the story and published it under a pseudonym.

BLACK KNIGHT

He was born with his left thumb missing, constituting a source of great pain throughout his twenty-one years. First, in grammar school and High School, and then in college, he was treated as a freak. He dreamed of becoming a physician, like his grandfather, rather than a famous (or infamous) trial attorney like his father. His family had roots that went far back into Louisiana's history. He was a St. Clair, and even though his branch of the family had dropped to lower-middle-class status because of his father's incompetence and asinine investments, he continued to be very proud of his family name. Pierre August St. Clair was named after his grandfather and cared little for his father, Roy. Pierre's mother died before he was ten, and the family fortune had begun to evaporate by that time. Fortunately, his standing as a "legacy" and his grandfather's endowed several professorships at Tulane University assured his access to a college education. While not bright, Pierre was tenacious and liked to read, and, as a result, his grades at Jesuit High were excellent. He entered Tulane without the typical problems students encounter in the first years of college. Pierre August moved out of his father's home to reside in the New Orleans French Quarter, where he could submerge himself in a bohemian atmosphere while studying without his father's intolerable presence.

For three years, Pierre took pre-med requirements receiving A's in most of his classes, so he was convinced that medical schools would compete to have him attend their program. To his dismay, the Chair of the Department of Zoology, Professor John Kent, on whose recommendation Pierre was counting to enter medical school, informed him that Pierre's handicap was an insurmountable stumbling block and that Kent could not write a letter on his behalf. Pierre was devastated: a whirlpool of emotions overwhelmed him, nauseating him so that he immediately ran out of Professor Kent's office to vomit in the nearest men's room. Pierre associated the spurt of vomit with the smell of violets that frequently exuded from a decomposing body, leaving a vile taste in his mouth. The white commode, stained with a brownish film, the remains of the jambalaya and black beans he had two hours earlier for lunch, overshadowed his consciousness and nightmares in the coming days. That incident changed Pierre's life. After that, he turned to literature and philosophy to escape what he bitterly considered one of life's many injustices.

Since his apartment in the Quarter was only a block from "The Seven Seas," a bar frequented by residents and students from Tulane and U.N.O., he became a habitual customer. The building where the bar was located had large windows with iron grille-work and high ceilings that kept the buildings cool and airy in the summers before air-conditioning was invented. Several feet long sign protruded from the facade of the white-washed wall: a replica of a pirate's ship carved out of cherry wood with the name "The Seven Seas" in burnt green on the gunwales, above two tiny rows of cannons. A bowsprit shaped like a bare-chested maiden extended forward from the stem. Inside the club, benches, stools, tables, lamps, life preservers, and other assorted oddities were scattered throughout, underscoring the nautical motif. Four tables offered facilities for playing chess. From the four hand-sawed wooden ceiling beams, bleached by time, hung four small light bulbs dressed with multicolored paper shades and red fringes— the pseudo-Tiffany-type shade sold in most of the Quarter's tourist traps. The smallness of the bulbs immersed the room in perpetual twilight that hung over the four chess tables directly beneath the Tiffany-shaded light bulbs. Pierre spent most nights playing chess at the "Seas," a game he had played with his grandfather since he was seven, experience placing him near a master's level. He sublimated the anger and hate he now felt for humankind by defeating almost everyone that challenged him. Pierre

August St. Clair had decreed that ethics and morality were irrelevant and laws of society likewise. Before his traumatic conversation with Professor Kent, Pierre was relatively self-conscious about his handicap; afterward, he embarked upon an obsessive sojourn to hide his missing extremity. He had a black glove made with a false thumb and wore the glove at all times, while keeping the hand in his pocket whenever possible. While playing chess, however, Pierre kept that hand visible and, as a result, he became known at the "Seas" as the "Black Knight." Furthermore, Pierre always chose black pieces as part of a strategy to devastate those who played him. Yet another vagary singled Pierre out from most of the other freaks that frequented the "Seas": he played on the jukebox the theme from "Elvira Madigan," a movie he had seen and liked. The music was Mozart's Concert No. 21 for piano. Because it had been the most popular record that year, the melody managed to carve a niche in the jukebox among the Stones, the Beatles, Bob Dylan, and Jimmy Hendrix. Pierre usually puts the coin in the machine and marks D7 before starting a game. The record somehow was played by the busy jukebox of the "Seas" within the ten to fifteen minutes his challengers generally managed to survive. One wonderful Friday, close to midnight, Pierre saw her for the first time. Most patrons had already fallen under the spell of alcohol or the drug of their choice (the Seas was a good place to score grass, bennies, and even smack). They were no longer interested in playing chess. Pierre busily scribbled impressions about the previous game in a notebook he toted with him and where he also wrote poems when the inspiration struck him. As Pierre August wrote, he heard Mozart's concert begin to play. Shortly after, one of the most beautiful women he had ever seen sat down before him and asked for a game. She was rather androgynous, with her red hair cut very short, a la Mia Farrow. He thought her eyes were intensely blue and the stereotypical bedroom eyes he had read and heard so much about. Pierre had little experience with women—he had only known two. As he began to think of her, the apparition had rosy flesh that glowed even under the dim cone of light that showered the chess table. Pierre recalled the pre-Raphaelite beauties he had studied in his art history class. She wore very little make-up and a western blouse, jeans, and a denim vest. The item of clothing that surprised Pierre the most was the biker boots with small chains strapped around them. He assumed immediately that she was a lesbian, part of the gay community residing in the Quarter. They played, and he lost for the first time in countless games. She (to be called by any name since she told Pierre to select one), Elvira or Elvie, Pierre's choice, would appear at the Seas every other week on average, playing a game or two with him before disappearing in the Quarter's enchanted nights. Elvira's outfits differed, but the motif and clothing were the same: pants, blouse, vest, and biker boots.

One Saturday evening, she informed Pierre Augustus that she had concluded that he could not defeat her because of a lack of motivation and that if he won that night, he could take her to his place and do whatever he wished with her. Pierre, a sexually inexperienced young man to whom women were a conundrum still to be deciphered, concluded she was mocking him but tried to play as well as he could, and he won. One can always wonder if she allowed him to win or if he played a better game that night. In any event, he was convinced she was being facetious. When Elvira told him I am yours tonight, he finally realized he was about to make love to his White Goddess. Elvie, Pierre discovered, knew a great deal about sex and those positions that intensified not only her orgasms but also Pierre's, and he quickly became an adept apprentice. Elvie's sexual philosophy was that anything was acceptable as long as both partners enjoyed whatever they were doing. Elvie preferred either the one thousand cranes position or to be penetrated in the anus. Pierre discovered two things about himself as a result of his affair with Elvie: he loved sex, and he was very well endowed. The affair went on for months. Since she asked for a key to his apartment and exacted the promise that he would never follow her nor try to probe her identity, he never knew when he would see her next: she would appear in the middle of the night when he was already in bed, or in the mornings as he was preparing to go to school, but never again at the Seas. As a result, while at home, Pierre spent his time wondering when he would see her again. Sometimes she would not appear for two weeks, provoking miserable, dark days of despair during which Pierre concluded she had found someone else. But then, there she was again, magically appearing before his bed in the middle of the night, while at a distance, one could hear someone singing the blues. Then Pierre was glad he was not blue anymore. Pierre August's existence was now divided into before Elvie and after Elvie. Before her, Pierre's life was meaningless—a bus ride taking him nowhere, merely existing; a state of inaction and, even behind every undertaking, every class he attended, every shower he took in the mornings, there was nothing until there was Elvie. With Elvie, he felt complete, and life held meaning beyond his most florid dreams, despite Professor Kent's refusal to write a letter of recommendation for Medical School. But the moment he most feared arrived before he was aware of it. Two months and then three passed, and Elvie did not visit him. In Pierre's recurring nightmares, she was walking down the Quarter's streets with another man. As he approached them, calling her name, she disappeared. Pierre would awake bathed in his perspiration, still calling Elvie in his dim, gloomy room. And yet, desperately hoping to see her again, Pierre August returned to the Seas, played chess, and walked down the Quarter streets looking at every female resembling Elvira. But the weight of Giant Despair was crushing him, and despair was inside him and everywhere around him. Immersed in the dark fog of melancholy with no one to rescue him, his chess playing was no longer outstanding, so he had to wait in line to play. He no longer attended classes and feared his nightmares so much that he slept very little. One Sunday morning, as he perused "The Times-Picayune" he had bought, standing on the corner of Saint Peter and Rue Royal, as the morning mist fanned about the Quarter like lost tourists, and covered the rooftops like a white sheet straddling old furniture, he saw Elvie's photograph on the front page. The story indicated she was from a prominent New Orleans family; a former Queen of the Krew of Rex, with two young girls and married to a prominent attorney. Upon finding them very intimate, her husband shot her and her lover. The story continued on page two. As he turned the page, standing petrified on the corner of Rue Royal and Saint Peter, he was astounded to see his photograph reproduced from his Tulane student identification. Upon reading the lines identifying him as the lover killed by the jealous husband, he dropped the paper as if it were on fire. A whirling Quarter wind playfully swept up the pages of newsprint. It carried them a short distance as Pierre August disappeared, leaving no trace as if he had not been there.

The following story, "Mister Lucky," deals with gambling and its nefarious effects on some people.

MISTER LUCKY

In my twenty-plus years of practicing psychiatry, the patient "Mister Lucky" presents a significant case study of a graduated march into insanity. Since the patient kept a notebook giving an account of his daily encounters with the slot machine, an authoritative basis allows one to summarize his perspective on life and the world around him. Thus we may use his written words and the taped conversations held throughout his confinement at Biloxi General before his departure and unfortunate demise. Medical jargon has been eliminated because the publishers feel that this monograph, the first in a projected collection of case studies, should interest the general public, who would better appreciate it if most technical terms were omitted. The enchanting power of his favorite machine is described by Mister Lucky in his notebooks as spiritual experiences: epiphanies, mystical episodes: he stared at the hypnotic wheels of the slot machine, those spinning little squares illustrating heroic and evil, real and unreal, cartoonish figures, and the flashing kaleidoscope of fluctuating, metamorphosing, multi-colored lights, listening hypnotized by the cornucopia of variegated sounds spewed out by strategically-placed speakers. Lucky's pulse began to gallop, and adrenaline rushed through his veins like a Formula One racer doing his last lap. The "high" became a mystical occurrence where he could virtually reach out and touch God and nearly understand His grand design.

The participation of chance was so clear and so subtle, just as inconceivable as his winning so frequently in that same penny machine he played every night. The slot machine gave him enough mini-jackpots to sustain himself with those winnings in Biloxi. But later, when his fortune changed (he claimed the device was doctored to keep him from winning), his depths of depression were unmeasurable; he described the low as falling into a bottomless pit. During those instances, shortly before he was committed, he would get up and walk away from the machine in what Mister Lucky described as an out-of-body experience where he saw himself ambling in a fog into which all the players in the Casino disappeared. At the same time, his stomach and his head fluttered like a demented whirling-dervish dancer. Mister Lucky had dropped out of Mississippi State University halfway through his sophomore year. Since he read very slowly, was dyslexic, and the sciences did not appeal to him, he found no appropriate calling among the many majors the University had to offer. Mister Lucky did not expect much from life. At age twenty, a wife and children were beyond his concerns, so he found employment as a salesperson in a women's shoe department at Biloxi's mall.

In the evenings, Lucky would go to Beau Rivage and spend a couple of hours playing the slot machines. He followed this routine for three years until the fated day when the slot machine of his life arrived. One April afternoon, she was among four machines installed in a prominent area of the Casino (adjacent to the buffet) as Lucky played nearby. Two slot machines were called Mister Lucky, and the other two were Ms. Lucky. The Mister Lucky machines had female voices that resembled Marilyn Monroe's.

In contrast, the Mister Lucky machines featured a male voice reminiscent of Humphrey Bogart. As a result, most men, including the patient in question, played Mister Lucky, while most women engaged with Ms. Lucky. The voices in question cooed with bedroom nuances whenever the player won over two-thousand dollars, "you are so lucky, Mr. Lucky," or, in the case of the other two machines, "you are so lucky, Ms. Lucky." The patient began playing one of the Mister Lucky machines and repeatedly won small sums. Whenever he won, Marilyn's voice praised him. It informed him he was a fortunate man while simultaneously playing the theme song of a popular television program with the same name as the machine. According to the patient, her silence was painful and bewildering when he lost, which was seldom. Mister Lucky's good fortune with the machine evolved over three years. During that time, he could spend up to twelve hours with the slot machine (usually from 9:00 p.m. to 9:00 a.m.) and be ahead by two hundred dollars. He moved into the hotel, and between winnings and comps, he slept, ate, and drank at the Beau Rivage. He won at least two weekly mini-jackpots of $500.00 and $800.00. Those amounts were consumed briskly by the room at the hotel and his meals at expensive restaurants. The winning of the jackpot was announced by the machine with Marilyn's voice singing engagingly with her bedroom voice, the melody of a song written expressly for the machine:

OOO! You're soo Lucky, Mister Lucky,
I want to share my life with you,
For I want to be lucky too,
Come, come to me now, my lucky love
and tell me, tell me you love me true!

All the machine lights would blink, a deafening cacophony would erupt, and then, a few minutes later, two blue-uniformed employees of the Casino would count out and place on the palm of Mister Lucky's hand the amount he had won in the form of crisp new bills, from which Mister Lucky would select one or two, depending on the denomination, and tip the employees. The cocktail waitress would rush to serve him a vodka martini with two olives, as she had been instructed when Lucky first started to win the noisy jackpots. She was unfailingly well rewarded. Mister Lucky became a minor celebrity, and onlookers usually watched him play and vicariously joined in his triumphs. It was uncanny that only he could win jackpots with that machine since most people who played the four slot machines in question lasted only an hour without beginning to incur relatively heavy losses.

It should be noted that the Mister Lucky slot in question was the only machine where Mister Lucky could win. Mister Lucky's Notebook entry for April 15 (which he called the cruelest month since he found and lost MM that same month) states that after playing for about an hour, as always with the machine, he heard sudden popping, saw a flash and smoke, and then she was covered in darkness. The technicians appeared from nowhere and worked on the machine most of the night. Mister Lucky was obliged to retire earlier than usual. Late the following day, after having a several-course brunch (eggs Florentine, eggs Benedict, grits, smoked salmon, fried catfish, and various fruits and juices), he began to play the machine again. Still, to his dismay, she did not respond. He sensed that she was no longer the same and that her soul had been removed. Lucky rushed to one of the security people asking for an explanation. He became agitated and abusive, was arrested, and spent the night in Biloxi Central Lock-Up. Upon his release Mister Lucky returned to the Casino with a hammer, battering and shattering the machine's glass. Lucky was arrested again and taken to Biloxi General Hospital, where he eventually spent a few years. Lucky's contention was that the Casino had used and exploited him by setting the machine to pay only when he played and thus attracting more players to the Casino who had heard about Lucky's good fortune. He reached a point while in confinement when Lucky realized he would not be capable of behaving rationally in the real world outside the Hospital, and he wanted to remain committed. Several unsuccessful suicide attempts were dismissed as Lucky's calculated attempts to remain interned. Unfortunately, with state budget cuts and worsening financial conditions, the authorities released Mister Lucky into the outside world he feared. Lucky returned to Beau Rivage immediately after his release and proceeded to play his beloved machine again. As in the past, Mister Lucky began to win, and a small crowd of onlookers gathered around the area. Everything seemed back to normal when suddenly, a flashing light erupted from the machine he was playing. Lucky's body twitched, his hair caught fire, and the man fell dead. Two eyewitnesses claimed that one of his legs became a goat's hoof as he shuddered while being electrocuted. However, the autopsy did not find anything out of the ordinary. Some people who have played the machine since Lucky's death insist that when someone wins a jackpot (which seldom occurs), as Marilyn's voice finishes singing her song and says, "tell me you love me true," a faint male voice responds: "I love you true." Myriads of additional details in Lucky's notebook and our taped conversations pertain to his life in general, although the vast majority concern expensive menus. Lucky described at great length the food consumed (he became obese during the years he played the machine). These commentaries lack any clinical relevance, as do his ramblings about his sex life (evidently, some groupies found it exciting to go to bed with Lucky). Although several statements about a male voice are heard from the machine, no ontological proof exists that it is Lucky's voice.

The following story continues with the gothic milieu which I will discuss later.

SHRINES

Raymond Ernest Robichaux, whose few acquaintances called him Ray, felt unhappy with his life. Raymond Ernest found himself counting the days until his two-week vacation. Raymond had been a pre-med major in college, graduating with a B.S. in Chemistry from the University of New Orleans, and had applied to several medical schools without success. Desperate and adrift for months, Raymond attended a job fair. While visiting one of the many kiosks with large signs filled with brochures touting the corporation's accomplishments and wonderful benefits available to the employees, he obtained information on a seemingly exciting pharmaceutical company. Raymond Ernest Robichaux applied for a position as a pharmaceutical rep for a well-known-international conglomerate. He accepted immediately when they offered him the post. He had to drive from New Orleans's French Quarter, where he rented an efficiency loft. His work area was limited to three states: East Texas from Dallas to Houston and Louisiana and Mississippi. Ray drove a Ford, which consumed very little gasoline and allowed him to save on his travel stipend. He stayed in cheap motels, saving the difference for himself. Most such motels had a faintly musty smell that reminded Ray of the odor permeating the oncologists' offices he so frequently visited. The musty smell was perhaps from the baseboards' dampness that never went away, eventually becoming part of the environs. Raymond decided to save as much as possible and resign in a few years. Ray Ernest did not care much for his job, which entailed visiting dozens of oncologists' offices, sometimes six days per week. While waiting to promote his wares, he had to witness a parade of unhealthy bodies that remained with him no matter how much he tried to erase them from his memory: Ray could not get the myriad of tragic figures out of his head. Pale, moon-faced women with no hair and bulging eyes like deer's frozen in the headlights; skeletal men with skin so yellow one could see the blood vessels beneath, like the road maps Raymond had to consult before memorizing the route that took him back roads and small towns. In some instances, the coughing and the handkerchiefs stained with blood turned his stomach so violently that Ray couldn't eat even hours after witnessing such incidents. Ray was not a happy man. His mother, Donna, an Irish woman, had left his father, Ernest, and returned to Ireland when he was barely ten. Ernest drank himself to death while listening to melancholy ballads from the fifties. All those songs lamenting how the lover had gone away inundated their apartment during Ray's teen years. By the time Ray was 18, his father had died from a heart attack and cirrhosis of the liver. Ray was abandoned by the love of his life, Sandy, while they were still in college. Sandy and Ray had been high-school sweethearts, notwithstanding their belonging to different social classes. She was from an old Louisiana family, the Landries, who were members of the Krew of Comus since the nineteenth century. Her father and mother had been King and Queen during Mardi Gras. Sandy had attended Sacred Heart School, a private nuns' school for girls. Ray's ancestors were Acadian and dirt-poor. Because his father had worked as a janitor for Jesuit High and Ray was very studious and bright, he obtained a scholarship at Jesuit. The Catholic girls' and boys' schools' Friday dances during the school year provided the occasion when Ray and Sandy met. He fell madly in love with her but never felt sure how much she loved him. While Sandy was a pre-med student at Tulane, Ray was studying pre-med at the University of New Orleans. Still, she was accepted by a medical school on the East Coast, precipitating the break-up of their relationship. Ray, bitter and obsessed with the notion that perhaps Sandy was as fast as the Beamer her family gave her upon acceptance into medical school, worried that he had been blinded by his love or hope that she would become his wife, not realizing how egotistical she truly was. Delving into the past, he remembered weekends when Sandy left campus to see her parents at their cabin in Bay Saint Louis, and he had been unable to contact her. There were also the parties at her sorority when she had danced with other men, much to Raymond's displeasure. Ray's childhood memories, which sometimes intruded into his consciousness like unwanted house guests, were his father's drinking and unhappy love ballads drifting from a record player. Since his mother's name was Donna, his father had several worn-out copies of the Ritchie Valens song by that name. Sometimes the words would come into his brain, and without realizing it, he would murmur those catchy words:" I had a girl, Donna was her name since she left me, and I've never been the same." Ray had inherited his father's record collection and transferred it to tapes. Masochistically, he now took them on his long trips, replaying those same unhappy love songs: Tommy Edward's "It's all in the game," The Fleetwood's "Mr. Blue," Roy Orbison's "Only the Lonely," Johnnie Ray's "I'll Never Fall In Love Again" and "Cry." After several months as a pharmaceutical rep, Raymond Ernest Robichaux began experiencing a recurrent dream endowed with vivid recall when he awoke, staring at the faces of patients from the doctors' offices. But now, they were flagitious, menacing, and grotesque, as though transposed from horror movies. Their eyes were fierce and bloodshot, with flecks of blood and foam covering their lips. Ray didn't actually begin to worry about his sanity until the heinous shapes began appearing along the road. Coincidentally, the phantom shapes appeared in certain spots noticed during previous trips, which he had mentally termed "shrines," places where a fatal accident had occurred and friends and relatives of the victims placed crosses, flowers, photos, or even toys if a child had perished. These shrines were few, far, and few between, but the stark apparitions were disconcerting enough to cause Ray to consider visiting a psychiatrist. He decided to drive more often during daylight if his eyes and the effects of darkness were causing the hallucinations. To his dismay, the figures also began appearing during the daylight hours. The ghosts, for he had concluded they were not of this world, simply stood there, apparently looking at him. When Ray saw them at night, the headlights added a dimension missing during the day when they seemed translucent. Frequently, trauma to the head and face had bloodied the features of the ghosts, and their limbs suggested those of dolls that children had cruelly deformed. Raymond Ernest Robichaux realized he must confront these demons, so he stopped the car when he next spotted the figures and rushed to the site on foot, often risking being killed by automobiles on the highway, the occupants of which often blew their horns and shouted profanities. To Ray's dismay, the ghosts disappeared once he reached the shrine. After such experiences, upon returning to his car, Ray's body trembled as if he were inside a freezer, unclad or overcome with fever. His stomach contracted with nausea, not so much from fear as the dread of the unknown. Ray fought the desire to remain, waiting for the apparitions' return; feelings beyond his control or understanding kept him there, not allowing him to leave or recover. Several phantasmal incidents later, he began to accompany his driving by low continuous humming, sometimes singing along with the taped songs, mainly to keep himself from thinking about the apparitions. Raymond was morose, suddenly weary and sullen, gradually drowning himself in despair with no idea what to do. A tsunami of emotions overwhelmed him. One night in the early fall, after a long rainy day, during his return from Texas to New Orleans, while driving somewhere between Lafayette and Baton Rouge, he passed Grosse Tete and Whiskey Bay when the fog rose from the bayous and filaments of angel-spittle—or still more relevant—of devil-spit were covering the highway, another ghostly figure materialized on the wide shoulder of I–10. He had been listening to Johnnie Ray's "Cry." As he sang along, "when your sweetheart sends a letter of goodbye …" his eyes moistened and blurred like his vision of the pavement, the trees, and the brush outside, reliving the letter from Sandy terminating their relationship. The figure on the shoulder of the road looked so familiar that he stopped and ran back into the cold evening drizzle, drawn irresistibly to the apparition. As Raymond reached the place, something extraordinary happened: the figure did not vanish this time. Examining it closely, he discovered, to his stupor, that it looked very much like himself covered with blood, the skin white as chalk and the vitreous eyes wide open. Panic-stricken, he fainted, awakening in an ambulance with the siren echoing the pain tearing through his head and most of his body. I pulled Ray's crushed, bloody body from the wrecked Ford. He barely had time to speak and recount his experience before he died as we arrived at Baton Rouge General, where I work. Ray gave me his pocket diary, asking that I tell his unlikely story. The diary provided additional information Ray had not had time to reveal. Despite the story's implausibility, I feel that Raymond's last request obligates me to repeat it.

Some stories dealing with supernatural forces were published with the title *Gothic Stories*. I am copying the original typewritten manuscripts because I do not have a print copy of the book, which probably had more stories. I found another story that deals with the uncanny, dedicated to Keats and written much later. The other story deals with his sexual adventures in the Quarter. The following two stories are the last ones I found among Fred's papers.

SANS MERCI

"And I awoke, and found me here
On the cold hill side."
"La Belle Dame Sans Merci"

– John Keats

I was residing in the French Quarter (it has Spanish-style architecture, actually) in New Orleans for a few months, trying to find myself. To my father's disappointment, I received a B.A. in English from L.S.U. in Baton Rouge. I was his only son, and I had broken the long family tradition of physicians. My father, his father, and his grandfather had medical degrees from Tulane; my great-great-grandfather was one of Tulane Medical School's founders—the doors would be open for me if I wanted to follow in their footsteps. My first year was outstanding: I had an A in all my courses, and Chemistry and Zoology, the classes I needed for Pre-Med, were also painless. Unfortunately, I took Comparative Anatomy, a required class my sophomore year. The lab classes, which met three afternoons a week, were rather curious with an endless dissecting of worms, fish, a frog, and several small animals until that cursed morning, I found the corpse of a cat on the dissecting table. Of course, it was a female, a calico cat with fascinating markings I had never seen on a calico. I froze and left the lab, never to return: I always had a weakness for cats since I was a little boy, and my parents always supplied me with at least two cats while growing up and into adulthood—my mother was also very fond of the felines. I suspect I developed the affection from watching her playing with the cats. I also witnessed numerous births in our garage, with many litters appearing like magic before my innocent child's eyes, and then watching those we kept, growing until their deaths either by old age or due to a myriad of accidents. My favorite one, I still remember, was run over by a car. She appeared in our backyard, bleeding from her mouth as I played with an airplane model. I was making it sail dangerously over the branches of the magnolia trees growing in the expansive patio of our mansion a couple of blocks from the Tulane campus. She rested at my feet as she took her last breath, shuddering as if she were cold on that New Orleans summer day. I was horrified and began to cry as I held her in my arms, trying to resuscitate her by talking gently to her and asking Calita to wake up. Such traumatic events remain with me. The moment I saw the calico on the dissecting table, the entire experience came rushing back. It hit me as a defenseless quarterback whacked by a linebacker. To my father's disappointment, my decision to major in English and write poetry for a living was decided then. My mother understood how I felt, so she decided to stay out and let my father and I resolve what turn my life was to take. After all, there were English teachers and failed writers in her family who wrote a great deal and were ignored by critics and the public. They were successful in the classroom, but their poetry and fiction reached very few. I'd rather not talk about my mother's forebears at this time because my father's bloodline is more relevant to this life story. During the War of 1812, after the Battle of New Orleans, which took place in present-day Chalmette, my great-great-grandfather, Frederick Henry Peters, who was a British physician with the 14th Light Dragoons, was taken prisoner and placed in a cell in a building in what it is today the Court House in the French Quarter. A young female Creole who was seventeen during that time brought food and water to him. He was allowed to leave the imprisonment after three months, stipulating that he would return to Great Britain immediately.

However, being a physician was an asset to the men who governed the city. They found a law that stated that a foreigner could obtain permanent residency if he married a Louisiana citizen. My great-great-grandfather decided to marry his warder since he had nothing in Great Britain. His jailer was beautiful and made love, unlike any British woman he ever had. Oshun was young, lovely, and had a French mother and a biracial father with Cuban roots. Her parents were financially independent and had an herbs shop in the Quarter that sold the best honey in town. Most of this information I have taken from family albums and the family history, carefully written by a family member every generation, and some newspapers from those years available in the family library—mostly writing about Mardi Gras. Oshun's parents were well provided for by their shop. The family was well-liked and tolerated by the upper circles of New Orleans's society. Her father had a very interesting ascendance; he was born in Cuba, and his Catalan mother had married an African physician. Such heritage made him exotic and tolerable, mainly because his French wife was well-liked. There is a fascinating story about them that I do not know much about. During the first Mardi Gras in 1856, she contributed to the floats' plans because of her carnival experience. She had been involved as a designer in a few in Nice, France (where she was born). F.H.P., my great-great-grandfather, by marrying the daughter of this well-regarded family (although they were not considered equals by any means), influenced the acceptance of the British physician into the New Orleans society. And facilitated a great deal; undoubtedly, my great-grandfather (Frederick Hunter Peters) married a wealthy society woman around 1884 (he was around 24, and she was 17).

The British physician (Frederick Henry Peters) had seven children. The oldest, Frederick Hunter Peters, was the first child of four men and three women and the only one in the family who attended a medical college in 1877, founded in 1834 and became a comprehensive university in 1847 by the name of Tulane University. The oldest grandson of the British physician was born in 1886 and had seven siblings; as expected, Frederick Harrison Peters, the primogenitor, attended Tulane and became a physician. He married into the New Orleans society and had a special place during Mardi Gras. Everyone in the family was a member of the Krewe of Comus. My father was born in 1915 and married my mother in 1940, eighteen, and her first year at Newcomb College, while my father attended Tulane medical school. I was born before my mother graduated from Newcomb, so she returned to finish after my birth. Unfortunately, because of complications with my birth, my mother could not have any more children. As one can see, my father was desperate because no other child could continue the family tradition—not even a female! My father's full name is Frederick Heck Peters, III.

My father feared my hypersensitivity, as witnessed by my reaction to the calico cat's death when I was a child. In those days, medical schools did not accept any deviation from society's established norms, so the possibility that I could be homosexual troubled him greatly. As a result, he decided that a sexual experience with a woman when I was fourteen would prevent or impede any sexual interest I could develop in other men. We had a cook/household manager in our house that my father had hired around 1941. She was taken to the hospital when my father was on duty with severe injuries from her lover. She had been kicked several times on her stomach to make her abort. Her white lover was married and did not want any difficulties with his wife, who kept him. She was the chef's assistant in a restaurant in the Quarter, and the manager had forced her to have an affair with him when she was single and about 21 years old. The man eventually ended up in jail, and my father hired Bonuta, Bonu, Bona for short, to be our cook. She also hired and fired the maids who took care of the house's many rooms and occasionally looked after me. I always wondered about Bonu; she did not have a boyfriend when the manager forced her to be his lover, and there were no more men after that. Although she probably became sterile after the forced abortion, her internal problems resulting from the blows she received in her stomach could be a fundamental reason. However, I suspect she preferred young women since we had a parade of maids at the house. The service quarters (slave quarters in a not-too-distant past) were separated from the house. It consisted of a rather large room with two double beds, a vanity, two large armoires, and a large bathroom with a tub and a shower.

I knew that room well since I had spent so much time there since childhood. When my parents left, she would take me to her room and allow me to play with her beautiful large breasts—I suckled them until their large nipples turned red. I never knew Bonu's origin, but she apparently had African blood. Bona was extraordinary: She could hold a cup of champagne on her buttocks standing up. I am convinced she was either Cuban or Puerto Rican. Whenever my parents took a trip for several days, Bona had me sleep with her and had the maid sleep in my room. Bona told me how amusing it was when my father asked her to seduce me at fourteen since she had already "deflowered" me long before. This made it easy for us to have sexual encounters since my father's awareness allowed us more freedom. I had no idea if my mother knew of my affair with a woman perhaps older than she was. When I went to Baton Rouge, I always looked forward to my weekends in N.O.

So there I was, sitting on the front stoop. I was on the porch of my apartment on the corner of St. Ann and Bourbon. I enjoyed watching the tourists go by with my small notebook on my lap, yearning for inspiration to make the book of poems I wrote an award winner. Then, I saw her walking down St. Ann towards Bourbon. She was a beautiful Creole who no doubt was a Mardi Gras beauty queen to be if she had not been already. "Her hair was long, her foot was light, and her eyes were wild." She stopped, looked at me, and asked if I lived in one of the apartments. I responded affirmatively since I had an apartment on the second floor, overlooking Bourbon Street, which extended from Saint Ann to the next building. Across the street was Pete Fountain's place, and Cattycorner was a hotel built at the expense of an entire block of beautiful historic Quarter houses. My mother's older brother, André Robichaux, who decided not to go into business and live in the quarter writing, owned the place until he was murdered. My mother, her younger sister, inherited the building after his untimely death at the hand of an unknown assailant. My mother's ancestors, the Robichaux, came from Arcadia, settled in the Lafourche-Terrebonne area around 1785, and became landowners. André Jr. was the oldest of my mother's three brothers. My mother's father, André Sr., had a chain of groceries in Louisiana. The three men were expected to get business degrees from L.S.U. and help my maternal grandfather with the grocery chain, which was renowned and financially flourishing. André changed his major after his second year at L.S.U., as I did, and decided to get a degree in English.

During the years he attended, the English Department at L.S.U. was among the best in the nation. Well-known writers such as Robert Penn Warren had been associated with the "fugitives" and the "new critics. The Department also edited *The Southern Review*, an eminent journal where many Southern novelists and critics published their works. André took classes with Robert Penn Warren a couple of years before the author of *All the King's Men* left in 1942. The governor of Louisiana, Huey Long, cut the English Department's budget to enhance the football team's funds. Such a move resulted in an exodus of outstanding faculty from the English Department. When I attended, the Department was a shadow of its former self. André agreed with his father and younger brothers to be bought out of the grocery store business and purchased the building, which housed several apartments. My maternal uncle left the Ph.D. program with only the dissertation left to write, as a result of the governor's action.

On the corner of Saint Ann and Bourbon, the building had three floors, and he decided to live in the most oversized apartment on the second floor. The apartment had two rooms, a living room, a kitchen, and two bathrooms to go with the two bedrooms. It had a shotgun configuration, and the front door, which opened to the living room, was in the middle of the shotgun. To the left was the kitchen, and to the right were the two bedrooms. My uncle used one of the bedrooms as a study/office where he had bookshelves on three walls. He had an ancient Pancho Villa desk and a typewriter on a small table where he spent many hours writing unpublished works. The bedrooms and the living room had large, tall doors that opened to a balcony. It extended from the corner of Saint Ann and Bourbon to the adjacent building, away from Canal Street, on Bourbon Street. I turned his office into mine, adding and subtracting a few items. In his bedroom, I changed the bed and removed the paintings of nude men, some of them by Quarter artists (George Dureau is one, I remember), and replaced them with posters of Modigliani's naked prostitutes, some of Picasso's young girls, a large photo of B.B. nude, and some enlarged pictures of my cats, and some voodoo masks Bona gave me.

The beautiful Creole asked me a bizarre request: would I babysit her for an hour or two. I was puzzled. She showed me a sugar cube she needed to take immediately. She needed to take it because she had to attend a voodoo ritual a few blocks down St. Ann, away from Bourbon. She needed to take the acid before she went. She usually lost her head the first forty-five minutes after ingesting the drug. She needed someone to keep her from doing anything harmful to herself. It was only forty-five minutes, and she would leave and be forever thankful. I asked her to sit next to me on the porch's top step and began asking several questions I now realized were inane. I was not wholly myself at that moment: I had been smoking some grass, and she was so beautiful—a faery's child—she had taken my breath away so intensely that I could not hold a coherent conversation. Shuno was her name, and she was a student at the University of New Orleans. Her parents urged her to participate in a *Santería* ceremony, and she and her parents disagreed on the subject since she was an agnostic. Finally, she promised them she would attend the rite that would take place that evening at eight. Her parents wanted her to be liberated from the university's ills and professors, who taught her not to believe in the spirit world and forget her African roots. She had decided to walk the Quarter's streets and find a stranger who would guide her when she took acid and through the *Santería* rites. Upon sighting me, she determined I would mind her through a night of acid and ceremony. *O, what can ail thee, knight-at-arms, Alone and palely loitering?* So, we went upstairs to my pad. I introduced myself as we were going

53

up – giving her my second name only, my Acadian name: Honoré. My full name is Frederick Honoré Peters, IV. Still, I seldom use the full name as my father does when introducing himself to people. We entered my place, and I directed her to one of my five large cushions of five that are part of my furniture in the living room, and Shuno sat down on a large blue one. The cushions circle a rectangular table about four feet long and three feet tall. The table was pastel blue with many tiny flowers in all the colors one can imagine. In the large and small drawers, with faces of different colors, I had my stash with numerous pipes and a Turkish bong. She asked for water, and I offered wine, but she rebuffed it, saying: "lips that touch alcohol shall never touch mine." A poster in a Head Shop I had recently visited had a beautiful starlet I had seen in some B movies saying those words. I brought her water, and she placed the sugar cube on her lips and looked at me, and I saw her starved lips that I could not resist, and I kissed her and drank her sweet fusion, and we were in bed in the wink of an eye, and we made love with. *And there she lullèd me asleep, And there I dreamed—Ah! Woe betide!—The latest dream I ever dreamt, On the cold hillside.* She woke me up while looking at the clock on the bedroom wall and remembered her night's commitment. We dressed very quickly because I was expected to accompany her to the séance or whatever it was.

We rushed down Saint Ann away from Bourbon, turned left on N. Rampart St, and walked a few blocks towards St. Louis cemetery, one of the few ancient cemeteries in New Orleans. We entered a house with a stucco exterior facing the cemetery. The house had a hidden interior courtyard covered with a dark tent. In the middle, people were sitting on cushions before an altar. The horizontal altar was a table about six feet long, four feet high, and three feet wide. It was shrouded with a white cloth covered with several skulls and lighted candles, providing the only Light under the dark tent. The drums' soft sounds greeted us as we sat in some cushions too close to the altar and detected several devotees whispering greetings to Shuno. Two or three minutes later, a black man wearing a white vestment entered the room and began to speak a language unknown to me.

Still, I could detect a word he repeated endlessly: *Shangó, Shangó.* The drums were growing louder as the Priest moved around the altar flexing his knees and hopping—his entire body shivering as he moved about. He reached under the altar without stopping his movements and removed a live chicken which I assumed had been in a cage. The Priest continued his pirouetting as the drums seemed to intensify. With a pair of razor-sharp shears, he swiftly cut the chicken's head. He began to pour the blood as he danced, circling the altar on the people sitting on the cushions closest to the altar. The head of the chicken jolted onto my lap with a generous amount of blood. I got up as if stricken by lightning and rushed outside the tent and out of the house.

When I stopped running, I did not know where I was--the acid and the traumatizing event had affected my memory. I knew I was in the Quarter again but could not determine my apartment's direction. I walked around possessed by the night's events, trying to make sense of it all until I found myself sleeping on a bench in Jackson Square. *And I awoke and found myself here*; I remembered that my apartment was a few blocks away. The next day, I searched for Shuno and the house, but I could not find either one. Shuno had remained in spirit with me since making love to her. It was a new experience, notwithstanding my affair with Bona, who, until then, had given me the best orgasms I ever had. I never thought having more pleasure than those moments with Bona could be possible. I searched for Shuno every night after that without success. And thus, I am *Alone and palely loitering*.

GASPER

I woke up later than I had planned that Mardi Gras morning. The night before had been quite enjoyable since the current year has brought females from all over the world. I suspect they were seeking to be as liberated as they possibly could during carnival in New Orleans—an example of the benefits for men that stemmed from women's sexual liberation. The result was a large number of females available in the Quarter lounges to the male with the ideal characteristics. Last night I was the specific male for the women in the Quarter because I brought to my apartment two gorgeous females: one at ten and the other at midnight. What a night! But that is another story without the horrifying consequences I am about to tell you that this story brings. I hope, dear reader, you will not rush to the New Orleans Police Department with the information I am about to give you. I am Fred Peters, a prolific writer of fifty short stories, four novels, two monographs, and several articles on Southern literature: Faulkner and Robert Penn Warren. Unfortunately, I am a prolific writer at the age of twenty-four with very few, if any, readers: the horror of it! And I go on and on, and I shall go on writing until I get my fifteen minutes.

I was giving the last touches to my pirate make-up while puffing on a joint a la Bogart, and the quantity of smoke the doobie was emitting was out of the ordinary. I continued retouching the patch on my right eye and my pencil mustache. I flashed back to those females who had told me I had a resemblance to Errol Flynn as he appears in "Captain Blood" and "The Sea Hawk." The eye patch was my idea to give it an exotic touch which is not present in the films above. At this time, I realized the smoke was making a sort of figure in my bedroom ceiling. Bona had told me that in addition to water, fire, and other means to see the future, the voodoo visions also materialized in the smoke. I could now see, hanging from a noose, between whirls and twirls that faded and recomposed as if goaded by unknown air currents that I was unaware existed in my old apartment, a human head with reddish hair formed. The ceiling fan was turned off in my bedroom, where I was at that moment, so that there were no air currents. The image faded from the air and from my mind, and I continued working on my make-up.

When I went out of the building on Saint Ann Street, I was greeted with the usual shouting, instrument playing, glasses breaking that one would expect from Fat Tuesday. I walked down Bourbon toward Canal Street with a great deal of difficulty since the crowd was everywhere like ants in a disturbed anthill. It was evident that the number of drunks was already very high: some were sleeping, others vomiting standing against some of the houses, the singing groups were everywhere, women showing their breasts abounded, and some men were urinating in public. Again, it was the usual scene in the streets of the Quarter on Fat Tuesday. At a distance, I could hear Louis Prima singing "Black Magic" and decided to follow the music, which took me to the "La Casa de Los Marinos" a block away. It was filled to capacity: it was a sausage ready to explode. I managed to shove in, and some of the familiar patrons greeted me as I squeezed through towards the bar. The bar occupied the entire east wall, with a myriad of bottles resting on the shelves between mirrors. One of the barmaids saw me and immediately brought me a can of Dixie beer—my favorite. I gave her $2.00, with difficulty because of the number of people at the counter, and began to move around looking for out of town women. Barbie, the barmaid, knew me from my frequent visits to "La Casa" and my remaining until closing time, and she knew, as well, I was a good tipper—the beer's price was only a quarter. It was February 27, 1968, and I had yet to win the Pulitzer. It was a recurring thought that flashed through my conscious: it usually appeared when I was enjoying myself, and the idea of writing had been evacuated from my mind. The weed helped me set aside that quilt complex for not working hard enough—perhaps the result of belonging to a family of Tulane physicians going back to the early 19th century. Barbie was another story I had already written with an explanation for her moniker. I moved, with difficulty, to the backroom: it was enormous with a stage where they usually had spontaneous locals playing—at this moment a trio of guitar, sax and trumpet were playing. The room was semi dark to allow for quite a bit of contact to take place. In the past, I had seen gay man get broken noses when they made a mistake in the dimness of the room – darkness that incited depravity. Since this was Fat Tuesday, there was that boisterous trio playing, and the people watching were dancing, but it was more like jumping. As a result, there was a lot of *frotteurism* taking place.

I managed to stand behind a female somewhat shorter than me so that her rear was almost to the height of the fly of my silk pirate's pants. I began to jump following the rhythm of the redhead female, and after a minute or so, she turned her head and said, "I am Katie." I responded immediately with my moniker for Fat Tuesday: "My name is Jesse." She had a beautiful behind I could feel it moving against me, stirring my penis into a prompt erection. The noisy place did not allow for many conversations, so I asked her with my lips touching her ears if she would like to go someplace else. She turned around, gave me a quick kiss on the lips, and said yes as she informed one of her friend's she would see them at the hotel. There were three other females with the same outfit: a black beret, a mini red dress, black tights, and one of them had a "Santa Muerte" mask. As we went outside, the sun was going down with a blood-colored effusion that made everything around red. Her face was flushed, perhaps the sun's reflection, which made me fantasize she had an orgasm while we were engaging in *frotteurism*. She did not seem older than seventeen: I wondered how she was allowed to enter "La Casa." Then I remembered that they did not have anyone at the door examining identifications for age. There was an important item I had not noticed inside: it was a black leather dog collar around her neck with a solid gold tiny padlock: it went well with her neck—it was so flushed. She had the sort of skin red heads tend to have, and the black choker, about an inch wide, with the petite gold padlock, gave her a decadent appearance.

As we moved on Decatur toward St. Philip, where another well-known tavern, "The Seven Seas," was located, I gathered information about her as we walked along. She was a first-year coed at L.S.U., majoring in English. Her family had some farmland around Shreveport—I had noted the twang prominent among those from that area. She told me how much she enjoyed the University, Baton Rouge, and now Mardi Gras. Katie and some of her sorority sisters came to New Orleans and stayed at the Monteleone Hotel, and were having the time of their lives. She was a chatterbox, and then I realized she was speeding. I was curious, so I listened to her tell me about her first year in school and the idiotic hoops she had to go through to join Alpha Omega. When we arrived at the "Morning Call," half a block from "The Seas," I was considering coffee and beignets, but the crowd waiting dissuaded me from trying. When we arrived at "The Seas," one of the undercover cops was playing doorman and examining identifications. Katie suggested we go somewhere else since she was only eighteen and had been told (erroneously) the authorities did not enforce the age for drinking. We kept on walking until we arrived at Bourbon, where we turned left toward my place.

At the corner of Bourbon and Dumaine, a block from my house, was the Drag Queen Beauty Pageant site. The platform had not been removed, and a couple of drag queens were parading across the stage before a crowd of drooling drunks. On the corner opposite the venue was "Laffite in Exile," one of the oldest gay bars in the Quarter. We went in without anyone asking for identification. We sat in a booth; she ordered a martini, and I asked for a Dixie. It was usually dark in the booths-area of "Laffite," and she pulled what looked like a snuff box and dipped her finger took some of the white substance, and inhaled. She then offered the box, but I refused: grass and beer are as far as I go; and a little cognac on holidays when I spent time with my father. Since he is very fond of cognac, we greeted the New Year by sipping the best he could find. She began to talk very fast again about the English classes she was taking, which allowed her to expand her reading of American writers she had started in High School. The writers who had spent time in the Quarter fascinated her: she told how she was impacted by Walker Percy's *The Moviegoer*. At this time, I took the opportunity to inform her that I had an excellent cognac in my place, a block away, and that I would like her to give me her opinion on some of the short stories I was writing. While I was telling her about my stories and the cognac, her hand was squeezing my penis. When I suggested going to my apartment, Katie squeezed so hard that I cried out. We got up and proceeded to my pad.

As soon as we entered my apartment, she began to undress as she looked at the paintings and posters that adorned my apartment's walls. Some of them, together with the building, I inherited from my uncle (a gay man who was killed during Mardi Gras a couple of years ago). She recognized Angelow's "Sawkill Reflection" and surprised me that she knew more about the artist than I did. When we arrived at my bedroom, she was nude, leaving all her clothes on the furniture that led to the bedroom. She jumped into my bed, and I could see her radiant pussy; her labia, both majora and minora, were engorged with blood because of her arousal, and they were very moist as well: her pussy was ready for my entering. Her nipples were like cherries decorating her small breasts, and very stiff. We started making love and Katie had at least five orgasms in twenty minutes, and then she fell asleep. She had the typical redhead skin: her skin was flushed all over. Her pubic area was as bald as an infant's head, and her engorged clitoris was visible between her labia.

Her feet were tiny, with her toenails painted burgundy red. I also discovered that under the black velvet choker was a dark mark on her neck, which I was too naïve to realize what caused it. Since I did not have time to orgasm before she fell asleep, I was still very erect. I launched an appraisal of her beautiful body, and I wondered about the causes for her bruised neck. I got up and rolled a joint to smoke while I studied her. I noticed that the small purse she was carrying was open, and there was a folded rubber mask of "La Santa Muerte." She opened her eyes and smiled with the most perfect teeth I have ever seen. She asked for a drag and I went back to bed. She saw my erection, at which point she grabbed my penis and began kissing it: talking to it as if it were alive or as one talks to a favorite pet. She then proceeded to ask me if I wanted to sodomize her: I was very startled. Since I had never been asked to do that, I thought the size of my penis would not allow me to enter her. She got up and picked-up her dog collar from the floor, and I realized it was a strange device. The two sides that came to a full circle around her neck, connected with the little solid gold padlock that tied the collar on front, had two hooks to insert one's fingers. Then one would use it to put pressure across the throat and deprive the person of oxygen. Katie wanted me to asphyxiate her with her black velvet choker as she had orgasms (she used plural). She told me she was in Paradise as she gasped for air while having an orgasm; the deprivation of oxygen did something to her pleasure centers. It was called erotic asphyxiation, and it was practiced quite a bit by students at L.S.U. It should be noted that the four years I spent at L.S.U., I never heard of such games. She showed me how to do it after I entered her anus. I used some Vaseline, and it was an easy entry, to my surprise. One important rule was that "Yes" meant continue squeezing, and "No" meant stop. While I was riding her, she would be masturbating so that she would have two penetrations—twice the pleasure? I remembered Juvenal writing: "*lassata sed non satiata*"

It was like riding a horse with reigns around her throat: I was galloping on a wild mare into unknown regions. The orgasm I was about to have had been unimaginable before this moment—so I tried to postpone it as long as I could. Suddenly, she went limp, and I thought she had fainted because of her orgasmic frenzy. I withdrew trying to ascertain what was wrong. I was shocked to discover she seemed dead. Katie's body was releasing stool from her rectum and urine from her bladder. I was horrified. What to do? The garbage trucks were on the streets collecting Mardi Gras trash. I immediately called Bonuta for she had her own room and phone, and explained to her what was happening. My parents were out of town so she got into her VW and came to my place. Bonuta had been with my family since I was a little boy. In addition to cooking, she also managed the household. There was a long story about her origins and how she came to work for our family. She took my virginity at fourteen, at my father's request since he feared that my hypersensitivity was a sign that I was going to be homosexual like my maternal uncle.

I had a small garage – big enough for two cars. I would get there through a small passage between the two apartments that were on the ground floor across from the stairs that were located in the middle of the building. I opened the garage door, Bonuta parked her VW and we went upstairs to my apartment—she was holding a small case. I was in a state of shock and she was able to calm me down as I told her more details about my experience with K. She examined the bed and went to the bathroom and filled my bathtub (it had four beautiful silver tiger paws holding it), with warm water and poured a liquid. Bona lit some black candles with a picture of the Archangel St. Michael, and began a chant in some strange language (I could hear a name repeated frequently: Baron Samedi), as she cleaned K's body. We then proceeded to dry her and put all her clothes back on. We took her body downstairs, to the garage, holding her between the two of us as if she were a drunk we were taking home. We put her in the back seat of her "bug" and drove about half a block from the St. Louis Cathedral where we were able to find parking space. We could not park any closer, so we carry her again between the two of us, entered St. Louis, and placed her on her knees on one of the pews. Fortunately, there was no one around, and we left her there as if she were a devout catholic praying.

Bona took me back to my place, and she explained to me that K had been possessed by a Loa/Lwa, and it came alive only when she was being strangled. I thought of a succubus as she was explaining to me what K was. She left me and told me to get enough sleep and call her to talk about the next steps I should take—my building was cursed. I am writing these pages immediately after the events took place because I cannot sleep, and I fear the police could track her corpse to me...

There is a fascinating tale about West Texas written by Fred's uncle and published in the New South Quarterly in a very small edition. I discovered that when I went to D.C. to check the copyright office about Fred's and his uncle's publications. Most of their publications were usually in small edition with small publishers. As indicated earlier, Fred's maternal uncle was writing his dissertation under the direction of the distinguished southern writer Robert Penn Warren. Professor Warren was a well-known Pulitzer winner writer. He was published in the little magazine *Fugitive* and was considered part of the fugitive group of Southern writers. Huey Long, known as the "kingfish," hired him to be part of the Department of English at LSU and provided funds for the establishing *The Southern Review* which eventually became a very prominent journal in the USA. In 1942 he left LSU for the University of Minnesota as a result of budget cuts of the English Department and the *Southern Review*. Fred's uncle left the University and did not finish his dissertation. Parts of that manuscript were published and he tried fiction without much success. I found a manuscript of the story with small variations from the one published in the New South Quarterly. I believe the location was changed from Louisiana to Texas to keep the identity confidential.

A WEST TEXAS LOVE STORY

Eduardo Guadalupe Romero Martínez was born in Odessa, Texas, April 3, 1954. The city of Odessa is located in the Permian Basin in southwest Texas, not far from the border with New Mexico. For all practical purposes, it is a geographic and cultural desert where the wind blows unremittingly, moaning and whistling under and around closed doors, as the tumbleweeds move about like giant crabs looking for food, and the ubiquitous dust—a dirty-red film that covered everything like a shroud—that gave the town's High School its nickname: "The Red Dust Devils." Eons ago, sometime during the Paleozoic era, a small inland sea covered the area, its teeming marine life eventually decaying into a sea of oil that transformed the area into an iron orchard of drilling towers and made many of its Anglo citizens very rich. The region has only two towns of any size: Midland, where the oil executives live and Odessa (the armpit of West Texas, some have dubbed it), where the "oil trash," the roustabouts live. Odessa is divided by railroad tracks into North and South, with the Anglos to the north and in the southwest the Mexicans, while the very few African Americans reside in the southeast. During the movement to end segregation, Odessa devised a brilliant solution to the integration problem: designate the Mexicans as white in the south and as minorities in the north, thereby keeping the blacks at bay for many years. Eduardo Romero Martínez was thus born into an environment less than conducive to becoming anything but a laborer in the fields, maybe a mechanic or a janitor, as his parents and grandparents before him. But, contrary to the highest expectations and fantasies anyone could have had, he managed under the anglicized name of Eddy Rome to graduate from Yale and then Harvard Law School and become a millionaire by the time he was forty.

The story of Ed Rome, Eddy R, to his closest Anglo friends, a fascinating and complicated saga, cannot be told in a straightforward, conventional manner, instead requiring frequent digressions to account for his family background, his "making it," his brilliant career as an attorney, his life in Paris, his three failed marriages (he loved women, but his marriages were riven with quarrels and betrayals), and finally, his return to Odessa (his life an Odyssey minus the mythic dimension), last love and final demise. Edward's life illustrates Oscar Wilde's epigram: "In this world there are only two tragedies. One is not getting what one wants, and the other is getting it." Eduardo Romero Martínez's life is circular and would best be narrated by concentric recounting circles, taking as the starting point his mother and father: Gloria Martínez Marqués and Guadalupe (Lupe) Romero Heredia. I was Ed's professor of English when he returned to Odessa and decided to seek certification as an English teacher. It is evident that he underwent, as James Joyce would term it, an epiphany in Paris, and decided to return to Odessa and "pay his dues." We met several times a week after he was certified to teach English at Odessa High and had long conversations about his life. When his breast cancer was diagnosed, some two years after he returned to Odessa, our meetings became more frequent and information about his life became more detailed as if he somehow hoped that, by telling his life-story, he might attain some sort of permanence after his death: he wanted to justify his existence. Ed impressed me as a terribly lonely man. He had become a stranger to his relatives and too "foreign" for Odessa. Eddie's maternal family was, from the standpoint of the Mexican community, from a good background. Gloria's father (Eddie's grandfather), Bartolomé Martínez Obregón, owned a small grocery store and the family lived in a three-bedroom home on Ada Street. Bartolomé Martínez Obregón claimed to have descended from Spanish immigrants who came to the area in the nineteenth century. His light complexion and green eyes tended to set him apart from most Mexicans in the area. Gloria's mother passed away when she was born so the orphan baby was raised by her aunt, Gertrudis Martínez Obregón, her father's oldest sister. Aunt Gertrudis never married and stayed home helping "Tome" with the store. Gloria resembled her mother: a younger Rita Hayworth with cinnamon skin. While in the eleventh grade at Odessa High School, she had the misfortune of falling into the clutches of the school's principal, Stanley Monahan, at the age of sixteen. Although she was a cheerleader and very popular, Gloria was a young woman who needed attention since she received very little at home: her father and aunt were very busy at the store. Glo, as some friends called her, helped at the store after school as soon as she learned to add and subtract. As a result, Stan's attention found her vulnerable and one day after school, she lost her virginity in the principal's office. Since Stan was forty, and married, with three daughters, the affair had to be handled very discreetly. He instructed Gloria to take a lot of Home Economics courses, and when she graduated at seventeen, he found her a job at the school cafeteria which facilitated her staying after school ended. This lasted for the better part of a year until Stan's wife, Elsa, became suspicious and, coincidentally, about that same time Gloria missed her monthly "curse," as she called it. In this instance, however, she felt it was better to be cursed than pregnant and she and Stan began discussing their future. She was Catholic enough not to consider an abortion, notwithstanding her committing adultery. Of course, legal abortions would not exist for at least two more decades, and having one was both illegal and dangerous. Gloria had accepted being Stan's lover since she never had enough self-esteem to consider herself worthy of a husband and a family. On the other hand, the idea of having an Anglo lover, part of a society to which she could never belong, flattered her immature, insecure character. This information was gathered from interviews of friends and acquaintances, newspapers accounts of the subsequent tragedy and some imagination on my part, since Eddie himself was not familiar with all the details included in this narrative. In order to give a complete account of Eddie's tragic life, it seemed essential to include his mother's sad fate which somehow portends Eddie's demise. Stan and Gloria agreed (she acquiesced to anything he wanted) that she would marry someone not perceptive enough to realize what was going on. Unfortunately, most people had underestimated Guadalupe (Lupe) Romero Heredia all of his life, and in this particular instance that mistake would precipitate tragic consequences. Like an insect attracted to light, Lupe succumbed to Gloria's beauty without questioning the motives of the beautiful woman willing to marry him and, as a result, was about to be mortally burned. Guadalupe (Lupe) Romero Heredia had been born with a club foot and a slight hunchback (he seemed forever bowing and had trouble looking most people in the eyes). Hence, he could not travel with his father and nine siblings, to do the pizca of cotton and other crops, from Lubbock to Wharton and back, year-round. His handicap and related problems at school kept him home, helping his mother from childhood. Eddie always wondered about his father's club foot. There were two literary figures Eddie loved and wished he could meet in the flesh: Brett Ashley and Emma Bovary. From *Madame Bovary* he took the description of Hyppolite's club foot, the better to speculate about his father's. He wondered whether his father's deformed foot was Talipes Equinus, Talipes Varus or Talipes Valgus—did it go downwards, inwards, or outwards? Did his father's deformed foot look like a horse's hoof? Did he have a pronounced gait? Would there have been a chance that his children (which Eddie would never have), might be affected by such a deformity? Eddie's father, a very weak child and often ill, quit school in the third grade and stayed home to help with the chores. To make matters worse, childish cruelty knew no end when it came to Lupe's contorted foot. Classmates would snatch his orthopedic shoe and throw it around while poor Lupe limped from one child to another trying desperately to get it back. A circle would form, with Lupe in the center, tottering about to the rhythm of some anarchist composer's tune that only he could hear, as the children passed the shoe around and around chanting, cojo, cojo, cojo. It was Lupe's father, Hector Eduardo Romero Otero, who decided that the child would stay home. With so many children, his mother, Alicia Heredia, needed the help. By the time Lupe was born, the last one of ten, five brothers were over fourteen, and two of the four sisters who were over sixteen, traveled with their father picking crops in the fields of surrounding farms to earn their keep. As the others grew older and worked closer to Odessa and within Texas became scarcer, the family traveled farther from home, going to other states with more abundant crops and higher pay. Then Lupe was assigned the task of home-sitting, until he turned sixteen and found work as a janitor at Odessa High School. Two years later, he started working nights, washing dishes at one of Midland's most exclusive restaurants, "Glutece." His life was very Spartan and deposited most of his earnings in a savings account at 3% interest. Except the two or three times a year that his brothers took him to Ciudad Juarez, *para ir de putas*, as his brothers called the visits to the bordellos, he knew no woman and seldom went bar-hopping. Lupe was not exactly savvy when it came to women and thus a good target for Stan's schemes. Lupe had a gift much appreciated by the owner of "Glutece," Clifton Hampton. One evening, as Clifton opened a bottle of Mouton Cadette, 1945, something extraordinary happened. Clifton enjoyed playing host at the restaurant and loved to wear the garb of Sommelier with the chain around his neck dangling the cup used for tasting the wine. This particular evening he was decanting the wine in the kitchen and as he opened it, Lupe, who loved to watch the process, was taken aback by perceiving a strong smell of vinegar and he told Clifton. Clift found it amusing that a Mexican dish-washer could pass judgment of some of his most expensive wine. Upon tasting it, however, he discovered that Lupe had a refined nose, which he decided to put to good use thereafter. Lupe participated in the selection of wines and every bottle's bouquet was subjected to Lupe's discerning nose. As a result, Clifton became very fond of Lupe and decided he would make a picturesque Sommelier: Lupe's rather grotesque figure soon became an added attraction for the restaurant. His garb, the limp, and the tendency to lean forward, reminded many a customer of Quasimodo. Clifton loved to tell the story of the casket of wine and the two wine tasters. One of them declared that the wine had a leathery taste and the other proclaimed that the wine had a rusty, metallic taste. Those around them ridiculed the two tasters until finding, at the bottom of the casket, a key in a leather ring. Clifton felt that Lupe had the potential for being a similarly distinguished wine taster and decided to help him along. Stan's decision to marry Gloria to Lupe required the intervention of an old friend of his known as Bells. She was the madam of a bordello that Stan frequented until he contracted gonorrhea and decided it was safer to find a mistress. Fortunately, his wife, according to Stan, cared little for sex and they seldom engaged in intercourse at all. Bells, María Ruiz Torrealba, had been a very attractive, petite woman who amassed a fortune in El Paso during World War II. She moved to Odessa in the late forties when the bordellos multiplied like mushrooms after a rainy night in the El Paso/Juarez area. The sparking competition was too keen for Bells to continue charging the high prices she once commanded. She arrived in Odessa in her late thirties, and as is usual with prostitutes, was aging fast. Bells decided to open her own "house" and contacted four of the youngest girls she knew in Juarez, opening the only (and therefore best) bordello in Odessa. She was also a "Celestina"—or go-between (the name originates from a famous Spanish literary figure who served as facilitator between lovers, setting up illicit love affairs). Bells rented rooms by the hour for those lovers seeking a discreet place to meet. Her establishment also offered the only prostitutes in the Permian Basin, with a comparably young and beautiful assemblage. Their youth and beauty earned her bordello the moniker of "the nunnery." Stan Monahan's closeness to Bells made him party to many stories and adventures the young madame had experienced. One particular scam especially fascinated Stan: the sewing of the labia minores of young females to simulate virginity. Since female virginity has been so important for many cultures for centuries, ways to have the hymen reconstructed have been invented. A crude way was to use cat's gut to sew part of the inside of the vagina to obstruct the entrance of the penis and to cause some bleeding—enough to stain the "wedding sheets" and allow the groom the satisfaction of having had a virgin. But, not only grooms wanted virgins; the bordellos had clients who requested and would pay high prices for young "virgins," believing that they would escape sexually-transmitted diseases without needing condoms. They decided that beautiful young Gloria would undergo such an operation before marrying Lupe so that no one would question the girl's honor or purity. Customarily, the groom had the right to return a bride whose virtue was questionable and Stan did not want to take a chance with Lupe—even though he considered the janitor retarded. So glorious Gloria, went to visit Bells for the necessary "surgical intervention" a week before she married Guadalupe Romero Heredia. Stan served as the "padrino" and he volunteered, after Gloria had given Lupe her undivided attention during lunch and a few dates that ensued shortly thereafter, with everything initiated by gorgeous Gloria, that he would request Gloria's hand on behalf of Lupe. After all, it would have been very difficult for Lupe to receive permission from Bartolomé Martínez Obregón, Gloria's father, to marry her. Stan, however, with his standing in the community and his wife's fortune (she was old money from ranching before the oil boom), commanded respect. On June 30, 1953, Gloria and Lupe were married in the church of Saint Thomas and many relatives and friends attended the wedding and well-catered reception that followed—thanks to Clifton, the owner of "Glutece." Stan provided the happy couple with a small house on the South side—his wife owned a large number of the small ranch-style houses that dotted the area where the Mexican Americans lived. They would live rent-free with the understanding that they would do the necessary upkeep and maintenance. Stan took advantage of the opportunity to buy new furniture for his house and gave them some things that weren't too big for the two-bedroom, one bathroom, livingroom, and kitchen dwelling. He also gave them a 1950 Pontiac which only Gloria drove, taking Lupe to work at the school when they both worked and then at night to his second job in Midland. This convenient arrangement provided Stan with the means to see Gloria since she would pick him up after taking Lupe to work and smuggle him into the house without the neighbors' noticing. The garage was attached to the house and a door went directly into the kitchen, a very unusual feature for houses on the South Side which, if they had a garage, was detached from the home. The visits of Stanley Monahan continued for several months after the marriage and even when Gloria became visibly pregnant. Informants disagree concerning the number of months she was pregnant upon marriage. Some claim two months, others say only one. I have no way of knowing who was accurate, nor any idea of how these people acquired such knowledge. Some speculated Gloria had a confidant yet to be found. Interestingly, Eddie was born April 2, 1954, nine months exactly after his parents were married so that Stan's paternity becomes questionable. Eddie had expressed to me some uncertainty about which of the two was his biological father (a DNA test was impossible because genetics was in its infancy). Since Gloria was cinnamon-skinned with green eyes, Eddie's resemblance to his mother trumped the question of fatherhood. The adulterous love affair continued after Eddie was born and Lupe remained unaware that the "padrino" and his wife had a mutual understanding. The house became Lupe's obsession and he started decorating and painting it and remodeled the fireplace which was unusually large for a small house, covering a third of the west living-room wall—until then the only source of heat during the frigid Permian Basin winters. The house acquired central heat only and each room had a small air-conditioner. Lupe loved the fireplace and kept a large supply of wood in his back yard. He bought an axe, and with two of his brothers, would spend a couple of weekends in October hunting for wood. The axe had a red handle and Lupe kept it sharp enough to cut through the hardest oak as if it were a block of butter. One day Lupe returned home early. Some say he was informed of the affair his wife had. Others maintain that fate decreed the tragic outcome. Lupe caught them in the act—the beast with two backs—without their knowledge and proceeded to attack them with the axe. The photographs I found with the coroner's report showed Stan and Gloria sliced into several pieces. Some photos revealed numerous abrasions/contusions involving Stan's back, with deep cuts running diagonally from the right shoulder, across the back, to the left flank area. He was beheaded and one of the photos showed the trunk separated from the head. Gloria's corpse photos highlighted the separation of the head and the complete transection of the aorta and pulmonary artery near their origin at the heart, with the heart pierced several times. Since she was under Stan during the attack, she was not as slashed and diced as he. Lupe, in shock and covered with Stan and Gloria's blood, staggered outside where he was observed by one of his neighbors who called the police. The West Texas media covered the story ad nauseam, and I have gathered just about every written report of the incident. A week after avenging his honor, Lupe was found dead in his cell from self-inflicted wounds to the head. Evidently, he committed suicide by ramming his head against the wall, although another rumor had it that he was killed while trying to escape. Baby Eddie was placed in the custody of his grandfather and great-aunt who raised him for a number of years with the aid of Moynahan's widow, who decided to adopt the child and easily convinced his older relatives that Eduardito would have a better future with her. Lacking any explanation for this whim of heiress Elsa Gustafson, I offer several reasons for her fixation on baby Eddie: perhaps she felt obligated to right the wrong committed by his parents; it was a public exhibition of her Christian principles in the "buckle on the Bible Belt;" or perhaps more darkly (the rage of hell was reigning in her heart), to seduce the son of parent(s) who had betrayed and embarrassed her so publicly. Ed returned to Odessa from Paris, after his divorce from his third wife, Cecile, to do penance for what he felt was a worthless existence and proceeded to obtain certification for teaching English at the secondary level, volunteering to teach at a school located on the South Side, where blacks and Hispanics lived, and for most of whom English was a second language. While completing certification, Eddie began an M.A. in English and wrote a thesis under my direction entitled "Deconstructing the Deconstructors: John Fowles's *Mantissa* and *The Parody of Theory*." One of Eddie's favorite novels was *Mantissa* for he considered the novel an onslaught on contemporary theory and its misguided disciples. When Eddie's cancer appeared, it confirmed his belief that, as he had abused womankind, it constituted an ironically appropriate punishment, given the form of breast cancer. Eddie felt morally and spiritually despicable and believed that not even the disease could extirpate his loathsomeness. The first symptoms of the malignancy appeared as a discharge, suppurating like an infected blackhead, from the left nipple, which he initially rationalized as a blow he received on his left breast while opening the hatchback of his car. After several months had passed, and his white t-shirts continued to display the roundish, red mark of the suppurating left nipple, Eddie decided to consult his internist who immediately assured him that men did not contract breast cancer. Three years had flashed by (as he described his last years in Odessa and on this earth) since Eddie Romero's return to Odessa, and a year from the time his nipple began to discharge blood and pus, when he decided to obtain a second opinion. At this time, a noticeable cyst was growing around his nipple and the second doctor advised a biopsy which came back positive. Eddie's remembrance of the events after the physician said "I am sorry to tell you …," is blurred by the flurry of x-rays, MRI's, exams, nurses, physicians, hospitals, insurance forms, the same questions, telephone conversations that filled the following days and months. He decided that only with the M.D. Anderson Cancer Center in Houston would he be comfortable enough to withstand the torturous treatment awaiting him. Ed arrived in Houston one Thursday evening in January. It had snowed in Odessa so Houston's weather was pleasant by comparison. He reserved two nights at The Pleasant Inn, a place the Cancer Center recommended, which provided transportation to the Center early in the mornings. Ed saw very few people around and assumed the motel was not doing too well. The following morning, however, he encountered an array of somber, ghostly faces, holding large, yellow manila envelopes where most of their medical history was stored, while riveting their eyes on each other as they wondered what kind of cancer he/she had? Their eyes, Eddie would tell me, with a very dramatic gesture, were the eyes of death! Upon arrival at the M.D. Anderson Cancer Center, he realized again that he was not alone: hundreds of equally curious figures with similarly large envelopes milled aimlessly about, waiting to see their respective physicians, to learn what the treatment would be after surgery: Would it be chemo? For chemo one needed a subclavian "omega port" in the upper chest, below the right shoulder, connected to the subclavian vein so that the very toxic chemicals would go directly into the circulatory system. The injection of those chemicals into the arm would not be practical (they would burn the skin in some cases). Or would it be radiation, with which patients seemed to have returned from some exotic island vacation, but later, the skin peeled-off the area radiated like a banana, so that even to look at it became painful. Or would the patient have both procedures? Eddie had both: all the hair on his body washed down the drains of Houston and Odessa and his radiated area, like Philoctetes's wound, was an open sore for many months. The substances injected into the "port" included edramoicin, zytoxin, decadron and zofran and the nights and days following the treatment were filled with hallucinations heaved from Dante's *Inferno*, and he sank into the depths of despair. The only offsetting event during this period in Houston was his meeting Helen Harris, heiress to a cattle fortune from Amarillo, and Ed's last love. She was six years his senior and with her he lived the happiest last two years of his life. Ed met Helen that first morning at the Cancer Center. As soon as he saw her, Eddie said: "she intoxicated him with her pastel-blue eyes." The liquor metaphors were felicitous because Ed and I sipped brandy from Jerez and Cognac from France during our weekly chats. Eddie considered himself a connoisseur of life from bottom to top, and good liquor was one of his most treasured pleasures. Describing the meeting with Helen, he affirmed that as soon as he was close enough to speak to her, he noticed her ambrosial fragrance. Eddie saw her at a distance, standing against a pillar as the crowd gathered and milled around; their eyes met and she smiled. He approached her not knowing what to say, but as soon as he perceived her scent, Eddie felt he should comment on the fragrance. Helen explained it was a French designer's perfume (the tape was not clear on the name), made exclusively for her, and explained how she participated in the process of selecting and creating the scent. Their treatments coincided, so they saw each other every four weeks and after the affair began, they spent at least a week in New Orleans, in a house in the Quarter owned by Helen. Helen and her husband had had a mutual understanding as to their marriage even before she was diagnosed with breast cancer and, afterward, the breach was more evident and his (Daniel's) resentment of her worsened. Daniel had been a pretty-face dentist that Helen fell in love with after her third husband passed away and she inherited a fortune estimated at $100 million dollars, whereupon Daniel promptly became her fourth husband. A pre-nuptial agreement gave him a monthly allowance and One Million dollars in the event of divorce. About two years into the marriage, she became bored with him—he was no longer fresh and unpredictable, she would say to herself, and Eddie would quote her words to me repeatedly during the last months of his life—when Helen had already crossed over and Eddie was preparing himself to take the giant leap into the unknown. During my weekly meetings with Eddie, I recorded our conversations, allowing me to reproduce some of the most memorable quotes and anecdotes from Eduardo's life. Eddie Romero's first true love was Elsa Gustafson—the ideal oedipal relationship since there was no father with whom the child had to compete. Elsa was both Eddie's adoptive mother and his tutor (she had a degree in English from Wellesley) until he was fourteen and she then became his lover and mentor on everything she believed a gentleman should be, do, and know. Perhaps this abnormal relationship, as some would judge it, determined Eduardo's behavior during the rest of his life. Eddie was in Paris studying French in June 1973 when Elsa was hospitalized for a bad fall while tending her roses in the back yard of her mansion; she felt that those roses that her mother and grandmother had developed through decades to acquire an almost olive-green coloration, were hers alone to touch. Eduardo had been staying with a Parisian family that the "Yale Summer in France" program had assigned to him. It had been a long weekend because since that Monday had been a holiday, classes the Friday before were cancelled as well. He had studied French in high school and continued it as a minor at Yale. The fastest manner, he thought, to obtain the hours for the minor was to go with the Yale's Foreign Program in Paris. Furthermore, he was using Paris as a base for his "European experience." That long weekend he had traveled to Helsinki by train with stops on route in Berlin and Copenhagen. Upon his return to the apartment (one of those twilights tinged with red so typical of summer sunsets in Paris, Ed commented), Madame Swifan handed him a telegram from Odessa. There were only four words: "Mother ill/come home." It was signed by Glenda, one of Elsa Gustafson's three daughters. The following day Eddie was on his way to Odessa arriving on Tuesday and going directly to Odessa General Hospital where Elsa had been taken. He contemplated the most appalling sight his eyes had ever beheld: varicolored wires and disparate tubes connected Elsa to a myriad of machines monitoring and administering medications to her emaciated body to keep it alive. She opened her eyes a minute or two after he arrived and, upon seeing him, whispered "Eduardo." He held her hand for what he felt was too brief a moment hoping to communicate with her, but she seemed to drift into unconsciousness every other second. As he was leaving at the end of visiting hours, the attending physician informed him there was no hope. Because of a fall in her backyard, she was hospitalized, contracting a deadly infection. Ed went home to sleep, and the next morning he was awakened by one of the maids with the news that the Señora Elsa had passed away. Eddie felt that the inside of his body leaped outside and became like a sock inside out but, most distressing, the intense pain burned a hole in his soul. Ed reminisced about Elsa's death frequently, and confessed to me that even so many years after Elsa's passing, he continued to feel the intense pain of the morning the maid came with the message: the remembrance incinerated his soul. He felt like a bull stabbed several times by a clumsy matador. His woebegone expression in the mirror, which Eddy could not help but confront as he shaved that morning, reminded him of the time when his beloved "pantera," a mixed breed dog, was hit by a speeding car. I can imagine the teary olive-green eyes that drew women to him. My belief is that Eddie dreaded falling in love because of the difficulty of enduring separation from a loved one. Eddie went for a long run that morning, circling the outside perimeter of the campus of The University of Texas of the Permian Basin, some two miles in length. He began running at 9:00 a.m. and was still jogging around at noon, when the temperature was close to 105. Ed told me that his face was covered with perspiration that flowed like a fountain, tears gushed from his eyes, mucous streaming from his nostrils, and that there was a point when he thought his tears had stopped flowing. At that moment, as he ran across the "Buffalo Wallow," he saw Elsa crossing the street, waving at him, he waved back as he tripped and fell into unconsciousness. Ed awoke in the hospital to confront bewildered faces of family and friends gaping at him. The next day, Ed was already in his room at Elsa's Victorian home, still suffering from the loss of his "mother" and wondering about God and the universe. He had read Camus's *The Stranger* his senior year in high school and thought he could react very much like Mersault after hearing about the death of his mother: "Mother died today. Perhaps yesterday." Deficient in his self-awareness, he came to understand by Elsa's untimely death that love was a perilous feeling that one must learn to control. But most importantly, he understood, with the advantage of hindsight, that his suicidal run represented his threnody, his mourning Elsa's death. Elsa was buried the Saturday after Eddy's return with great fanfare, having been respected by the community for her many generous contributions to the city in particular, and the state generally. Ed had very little input into the funeral and was not asked to share his memories of Elsa with those present. He did not mind, Eddie told me one night reminiscing about the funeral, one of the biggest events that year in the Permian Basin, because he realized he would not be able to stammer a word without sobbing out his grief. The Monday following the funeral he received a note from Glenda, the oldest of Elsa's three daughters requesting a meeting in her mother's office with her sisters, Mary Beth and Lois, and their family attorney. The meeting resulted in a request from the three daughters to take a million dollars and go away quietly (their eyes, according to Ed, were like their father's, a pair of rubber push-buttons). Although Elsa's daughters had moved out of the house when Eddie began living there at the age of seven, he mistakenly thought he was considered a part of the family. Their coldness when indicating that he needed to move on, was very disheartening. In effect, he suffered two blows: the loss of Elsa and the loss of a family. He moved to Elsa's Victorian home the day of his first communion. She had encouraged Ed's family to take him to mass every Sunday and continued to take him to her church when he began to live in her house. He attended Saint Ignatius, a Jesuit school in Midland, and graduated in the top ten per cent of his class, but with a great deal of assistance from Elsa who tutored him, particularly in the first two years he attended, after which Eddy did it all himself. But Elsa provided him much more than tutoring for school: she taught him the difference between ethics and etiquette; how to please a woman in bed; and with an uncanny awareness of pheromones, Elsa suggested ways of using his perspiration after strenuous exercise, in order to attract the particular female he liked, instead of using synthetic perfumes; how to dress properly—with a preppy touch; the difference between a Windsor knot and a double knot; how to play a good game of chess; how to prepare and order a good martini (after all, someone named Martinez had concocted it); and a myriad of rules for urbane behavior which he tried to follow his entire life. He also learned from her the joy of reading: if Elsa liked a book, she would spend an entire night finishing it. But, most importantly, Elsa accentuated his having to divest himself of his "brownness," since otherwise it would be very difficult for him to survive in a "white" world. Such was one of the reasons Eddie studied French and never learned standard Spanish. Interestingly enough, no one reminded Ed of his origins while at school; he wondered whether it was respect or fear of Elsa. But not until the first night she made love to him, did Elsa disclose the tragic death of his parents. From the first day Eddy moved into Elsa's house, when her three daughters had gone to college and eventually married, she considered urgent to erase any vestiges of brownness and suggested anglicizing his name. Elsa commenced Eddie's tutoring as soon as he arrived and that very night showed him how to arrange the table for formal dinners and explained the importance of good manners and civility. Having flown several times a year from the time she was six and her father owned a plane that flew all over the States and Southern Canada, she provided the same education to her three daughters, and around Ed's seventh birthday, he received the same privileges. Edward saw New York and went to a Broadway play by the age of eight, and ate at some of the best restaurants in the United States by the age of fifteen. Eddy lamented often, using a term popular in the seventeenth century, that "marplot cancer" was about to erase all those marvelous memories of his childhood. From Elsa he learned to love one lover at a time and from his uncles he learned to regard women as sex objects. A distant uncle took him once to a bordello in El Paso where Eddy developed an aversion to prostitutes after observing the squalid conditions and later acquired the fear of venereal disease that Elsa instilled in him after she discovered the outing. Feel them, fuck them, and forget them was the relative's philosophy which Eddy somehow adopted. Make women happy so that when you whistle, they will run to you, was Elsa's credo. Ed amalgamated both, having one woman at a time and avoiding relationships he knew would not last more than a night. Ed was most women's ideal man with his six-foot frame, a clear complexion and permanent tan, plus olive green eyes which, some women had told him, undressed every female he scrutinized. From the time he was "BMOC" in high school, the quarterback of a mediocre football team, to his first years in Yale, Eddy had numerous short affairs which he ended when he "fell in love" with another beautiful woman. Ed never provided much detail about his sexual journeys with Elsa, but I was able to ascertain, as he imbibed his French cognac, and the warm liquid traveled from his mouth, and teasing his palate. When the liquid ran into his esophagus a shudder ran through him, and not unlike Proust's madeleine, precipitated his memories of Sunday mornings at Combray. At one point is his late teens Ed believed he was truly the scion of the Gustafson family. After all he had been like a husband to Elsa for most of his teenage years. Elsa's rule was respected at all cost: only when Elsa and Ed were out of town, were they to make love. While in the Permian Basin, they were mother and son, rather than man and wife. Eddie was fourteen when Elsa embarked on the most ambitious sex-education project ever devised, preparing Ed to be the lover of women he became. Their age difference caused no problems. In other parts of the world, older women often seduce a young boy and instruct him as to how to please them sexually. Eddy learned about the "G" spot and how to insert his middle finger in the vagina, using the base of the finger to massage the lower portion of the clitoris, called by Elsa, the "Y" spot for "Yes" with exclamation sign. As soon as Elsa exclaimed, "Yes! Yes!," usually a couple of minutes after Eddie began to manipulate her "G Spot" and clitoris, he was to enter hard and quickly, and begin the love-making until orgasm. In the summer of 1968, at the age of fourteen, Elsa took Eddie to New York and made love for the first time.

They ate at "Lutece," a very elegant restaurant, where Eddie put into practice everything he had learned about etiquette: the clothes to wear, which fork to use, dealing with the waiters and busboys, and all relevant information Edward, the urbane fellow, would put to good use the rest of his life. Elsa ordered three courses: the appetizer was crab cakes, followed by a Caesar salad, and for the main course duck, in order to determine if Ed could manage without using his fingers. The two portions of duck came in deep oval-shaped blue dishes with Chinese characters and a drawing of two flying ducks, resting in a brown sauce and topped with some vegetable unknown to Eddie. Still unsure which of the many utensils to use, he waited for her to show him. Notwithstanding the many home rehearsals, he found far more spoons, forks, and knives than on Elsa's table at home. Hence, following her advice to watch his hostess and do exactly as she did, Ed elicited high praise for his performance at dinner. After the felicitous experience in the restaurant, they next attended a Broadway show, West Side Story, before returning to the hotel. The room was a suite with a sitting room and the bedroom had two double beds; the bathroom was as luxurious as the ones in Elsa's mansion. He brushed his teeth and got into bed before Elsa, looking forward to the next day went they would visit the Statue of Liberty and other sites most tourists visited. Elsa went to the bathroom to prepare herself and the room was left in darkness with only neon lights creeping through the window and providing Eddie with a view of a room filled with a kaleidoscope of clashing colors. Ed was extremely surprised to see, at first the shadow and then—reflecting all the colors of the neon signs—Elsa's svelte nude body before his bed. Elsa informed Ed, with the same matter-of-fact attitude with which she taught him many other subjects, that it was time for Ed to learn about sex. Whereupon, she slipped under the covers, helped Ed remove his pajamas and proceeded to instruct him how to please her sexually. Elsa was in her late forties or early fifties, Ed never knew her real age, and he confessed to me that notwithstanding her age and having had three daughters, her body looked as young as that of his first wife who was in her late teens when he met her. His experience reminded him of the song that describes hearing a hundred gypsies playing violins upon contemplating the loved one. Thereafter, he would look at Elsa and love and desire would overwhelm him. He always looked forward to traveling with Elsa and making love to her. During these moments, as he recalled Elsa and spoke to me in a soft monotone, a few subtle tears would escape from Ed's red eyes, glittering with cognac and the myriad of pills he was taking. The chemo had affected his kidneys and liver so that he had to ingest additional medications to keep those organs from deteriorating further. Edward's first wife was a student of literature at Yale whom he had met while studying French in Paris. Since Ed believed he had to be faithful to Elsa, not until her death did he dare to think about Brett Ashley Oxford as a potential lover. Charismatic, bright, articulate, he possessed the gift of small talk, managing to engage anyone in conversation about anything. He had attended classes in Paris with Brett and they had developed a friendship; when he ran into her at the library the Fall Semester of 1973, they were beginning their sophomore year at Yale. And just as with Helen Harris at the M.D. Anderson Cancer Center many years later, when he was facing death in the form of breast cancer. Ed was drawn to Brett because of her scent, not in Paris, but later when he spoke to her in the library. Ed recalled that her hair exuded verbena, which to him was erotic somehow, something voracious and passionate. Brett Ashley was majoring in English and Eddie had taken numerous courses cafeteria style making him very well rounded when it came to the humanities. He had taken all the required courses in math and science, but was unsure what to do about a major. Brett's father was a Professor at Harvard Law School and upon meeting him and developing a friendship, Eddie found in Roger Eastman Oxford, IV the father he never had, his relationship with Brett became formal and he decided to ask her to marry him and become an attorney. Brett Ashley Oxford had gull-grey eyes (ironic, steely, sparkling eyes that gave her a Mona Lisa look) and red hair (red-auburn as the cognac Ed loved) with a rosy, smooth complexion that reminded him of Elsa and exemplified the female appearance most of Ed's women were to have. Brett's nose recalled Kim Novak and her full lips were like Brigitte Bardot's: forever pouting and always offering a kiss. Brett Ashley was slim with very long, gymnast's legs, having devoted some of her time to that sport as an adolescent. Brett was five feet, ten inches tall without shoes and when she wore heels she was almost as tall as Ed. After a couple of dates to the movies, and a brief encounter in his apartment, the young people decided to move in together and the affair lasted two years before Ed asked Brett to marry him. A letter from her father assured his acceptance in Harvard Law School, although Ed's GPA was respectable and his LSAT scores were high, the fact that Brett's father was on the faculty assured his acceptance. The marriage was a private one and Eddy's relatives were informed but not invited as he had severed practically all contact with his uncles and aunts. His grandfather and great aunt had already passed away; no one he was close to remained in the Permian Basin, and he had terminated most contacts including school friends. Upon graduation from Yale in 1975, Eddie entered Harvard Law School and Brett Ashley began graduate work in comparative literature at Harvard. It was an ideal situation: both students at a prestigious institution with a nice income so that financial needs caused no distraction. Two or three years later, shortly before he began clerking at the Chicago Law Firm, Edward realized Brett was having an affair with one of her professors. During those salad days having an "open" marriage was the intellectual thing to do. He discovered Brett's discreet and brief affair when he followed her to the library one night due to suspicions about her demeanor and some dark marks on her thighs that she attributed to hitting herself with the car's door, plus her reluctance to make love as often as they used to. She did not enter the library that night, instead getting into the car of one of her English instructors (one of the professors she was considering to direct her dissertation). Notwithstanding his Hispanic blood, Ed managed to look the other way and continue the marriage until the year he went to clerk for Monroe, Naper & Blakely, a law firm with nine hundred attorneys in offices around the world and a third of them in Chicago where he worked six days per week and fifteen hours per day. That year was like boot camp to Eddie who had managed to escape the Viet Nam War thanks to Elsa's connections and influence. He worked fifteen hours per day and, sometimes, seven days per week. Only five per cent of each class of interns would make partner, and only ten per cent would be hired, so the competition was ruthless and the back-stabbing ubiquitous. Lauren Monroe, (subsequently Edward's second wife), was the granddaughter of one of the founders, George Jefferson Monroe, a partner and director of the mergers and acquisitions division of the firm. She was a very attractive blonde in her fifties, had been married a couple of times and had several affairs with the interns the firm hired every year. Since Ed had had several courses in business and almost enrolled in an MBA program, Corporate Law was dear to him. As Ed exorcized his demons during our conversation in those unforgettable Permian Basin nights, while sipping cognac and listening to Caruso, verbalizing what had been and what might have been, furtive tears escaped from the corners of his eyes and scrolled down his cheeks. He greatly admired the blind faith of his Catholic relatives who unburdened all their troubles, physical and psychological, onto the Guadalupana, or the myriad of saints in the Catholic firmament, accepting stoically their burdens regardless of the outcome: When positive, the Virgin, God, or the saints were to be thanked for the miracle; a negative outcome was the Will of God and his wishes, his design was beyond human understanding. Edward wanted to have enough faith so that the pain caused by the cancer that was devouring him with every passing second would be pacified and he could sleep easily without fear of the unknown, that eternal sleep that was about to descend on him. But it was extremely difficult to evade reality when the skin of his chest looked unnaturally bronzed, where the radiation was killing not only the cancer cells but also the healthy ones, and had a suppurating, foul-smelling wound recalling Philoctetes's wounded foot as punishment for his betrayal. Ed felt he had betrayed womankind and his cancer was just retribution. As a result of his working long hours in the building of the Law Firm, Ed saw Lauren frequently at all hours. One evening, close to midnight as he was leaving for his apartment, as the two of them were in the elevator, she asked him if he would like to have a drink with her. She was interested in knowing the opinions the interns had of the firm and that was an opportunity to do so. They chose a tavern about two blocks from the building called "Rick's Place." The decor was homage to Humphrey Bogart's films, *Casablanca* in particular, with walls plastered over by Bogie's posters, piped-in music from Bogart's films, and attendants in Arab costumes. Several isolated enclosures, fitted with curtains shaped like Bedouin tents, invited those customers who desired privacy and Lauren requested one that particular night. As the maître d', dressed in a black tuxedo led them to their booth, "As Time Goes By" was playing. The booth contained lots of memorabilia from *Casablanca*, with posters and quotes from the film, in large bold letters, scattered throughout the booth: "The Germans wore gray, you wore blue;" "Tell me, who was it you left me for? Was it Laszlo, or were there others in between? Or—aren't you the kind that tells?" "Kiss me. Kiss me as if it were the last time;" "Round up the usual suspects;" "We'll always have Paris." The last quote was particularly ironic in view of Ed's residence in Paris and his eventual marriage to a Parisian. The private enclosure held a small table with two chairs across from each other and, as they sat, their feet touched. Lauren did not stir. Eddy felt a tsunami of emotions overtaking his body. Later, as they sipped martinis and chatted about the firm, she removed her shoes, placing her right foot on Ed's lap. Whereupon he massaged her black-stockinged foot while placing it on the erection he had had since arriving at the tavern. They left Rick's place and went to Ed's apartment where they made love, repeating these evenings often thereafter. Eddie told me, remembering that night and quoting another of Bogart's films, that notwithstanding their conversation, which had concerned mostly business, his plans for the future and other interns (since she was interested in obtaining the best of them for the firm), was for him a romantic experience because of the music: "You can say much more with a few bars of music than a basketful of words." Ed feared that his life, all he had observed and experienced, risked disappearing like tears in the rain, so I became his confidant and thus his amanuensis. Edward was hired by Monroe, Naper & Blakely a year later and shortly thereafter divorced Brett Ashley. He became a star in the firm and in two years he rose to partner and married Lauren. Those were his salad days, hobnobbing with the high society of Chicago, married to one of the most powerful women in the city and wealthy beyond belief. Very few could say he did not have the credentials since his degrees from Yale and Harvard were invaluable and his work ethic earned millions for the firm in two short years. He was a genius when it came to mergers and acquisitions and, naturally, a despicable bastard to some but a hero to those he provided the leverage to attain immeasurable riches. Ed was ruthless when it came to design the necessary maneuvers to secure the expected results, caring nothing about widows or orphans and pensions for old men who constituted obstacles to desired harvests. He became a notorious corporate raider. The Law Firm had a small office in Paris which Ed and Lauren visited during a month of honeymooning in Europe. They decided then that Edward should spend a couple of years developing the firm's interests there by hiring for expansion in the economic environment that the European Union would soon provide. Edward would travel to Chicago and spend long weekends with Lauren and managed, thanks to his hard work and business virtuosity, to turn the Paris Office into one of the most productive of Monroe, Naper & Blakely. However, the living arrangement took a toll on Eddy's marriage and after some ten years it ended abruptly. His third marriage with a French woman, Cecile Parrottin, flopped some three years afterwards—Cecile was half his age chronologically, but much more sophisticated and mature than he— Eddie decided to return to Odessa in the early nineties after what he called his "long journey into night": For several weeks after Cecile left him, he drank himself into a stupor with absinthe and pastis, forcing himself to vomit copiously. He described the nausea and vomiting as an exorcism to expel his demons. He would go to either the "Café Mably" on Boulevard de la Redoute, or two of his favorites in the Beauvoisis district: "Café des Bretons" and the "Bar de la Marine," order his drinks and listen to the music these establishments provided their patrons. It was usually jazz featuring numerous black female singers. One of his favorite songs was the one that had the following verses: "One of these days, you'll miss me honey," and he would sink into the depths of despair, guilt, and self-pity, progressively deeper as he downed the combination of absinthe and pastis (gulping a glass of each in turn, seldom reaching eight), and by the time eleven came around, he had already vomited a pair of demons and his clothes and breath exuded a foul stench. Thanks to his large tips and his being a discreet drunk, he was never barred from any of the cafes. One evening while vomiting in the men's room of "Café Mably," imagining his insides about to erupt from his mouth and remembering his second wife whom he had betrayed so ignominiously, he experienced a vision of himself in Odessa helping other Mexican Americans. Cecile had been the result of his mid-life crisis and prolonged stays away from Lauren, the typical man of a certain age falling in love with a woman much younger than he. While living in Paris he was asked to teach a class on Corporate Law at the Sorbonne. The first day of classes she was sitting on the front row of a large auditorium and, upon seeing her, Eduardo told me, he immediately recalled, like a teenager in love, Romeo's words: "What light through yonder window breaks?" He perceived a halo around Cecile's head and was immediately intoxicated with her looks: Very short red hair, rosy flesh and blue eyes that seemed to question, ironically, every word Ed said in his halting French. One week into the semester they had their first date and, soon thereafter, a passionate affair began. As a Francophile, Ed believed that French was the ideal language for foreplay and bedroom chatting. He loved it when Cecile whispered in his ear dirty sweet nothings. Cecile's wealthy parents did not object to her having an affair and eventually marrying Ed. Edward, having heard rumors of his wife's affair with a new intern and seeing each other so seldom after a few years of marriage, fortified his rationalization for the affair and the eventual divorce. Unfortunately, to Ed's distress, Cecile absconded from their penthouse taking only the golden toothbrush handle he had bought her for her birthday at Tiffany's. It had several precious stones encrusted and he obsessively recalled how the stones reflected the sun-light coming through the window as he watched his White Goddess's nude body, with a derriere that was a sodomites dream. Many mornings in Paris, while she brushed her teeth her beauty dazzled him. The rest of his gifts, all her clothes, shoes, jewelry, everything remained. If Cecile had not left him a note, he would have wondered if something terrible had happened. Her note was brief and cold: "Ed, I am moving in with a girlfriend. Adieu." Simone was an old friend of hers and a rather homely woman, according to Ed, who saw her socially, could never imagine that Cecile had such terrible taste: to leave him for such an individual. He felt that if Simone had been a man, he had ways to deal with it. If there was anything sexual between Simone and Cecile, he had no idea as to how to win Cecile back. The last three weeks of Eddie's life depressed me enormously. Our final nights together, although we met more often, were limited to my staying a few minutes while he rested on his bed, and naturally we spoke little as he was so emaciated from the cancer that overwhelmed his body, making his face and body a grotesque parody of the muscular, handsome Edward. His permanent tan complexion had turned chalky and his beautiful eyes were sunken and had lost their sparkle: It seemed like looking into muddy waters down a dark well. Wealth allowed him to hire several nurses around the clock at home. My visits were moments of joy for him, but he was too medicated to sustain a conversation for very long. At times he would sing or mumble old songs from the Catholic mass ("He will raise me up on the last day …") which seemed to give him peace. The last week of his life, after I informed him that Helen Harris had passed on (they had stopped seeing each other several months earlier), he asked for a priest. I immediately contacted Father John (I believe that's his name) at Saint Catherine to visit Ed and give him communion. A few days later, one of the nurses called to inform me that Ed had expired in his sleep. I think my nightly conversations, our tête-à-têtes, provided the best moments in my life, for he had lived well if not very long. I could never have afforded to visit all the places on the planet Ed visited, or to enjoy his business experience and women, but vicariously savored those unattainable pleasures. I have lived my entire life in West Texas and I am an Ab.D. finishing my Ph.D. at Texas Tech University. Unfortunately, it has taken longer than usual due to duties at my present position at the University of Texas of the Permian Basin. Other than attending professional meetings in different cities in the United States, I've never enjoyed the pleasure of traveling abroad. It seemed my duty to provide the world with Edward's insights into life as well as what I learned while listening to him so many nights in Odessa. Ed was truly insecure with a pathological need for approval and repeatedly wished and hoped that after his death, he would be remembered often, with kindness. Hopefully, the present text may fulfill Eddy R's last wish.

I am still determining how long ago the pandemic emerged. It has been more than ten years, probably. Nothing has changed: the drizzle continues to drip and drop, and the sun has disappeared. Mother Earth is retaliating for the damage humans have caused the environment. I have been traveling around the country, and it is all the same: the weather, the cars scattered on the highways, the streets filled with detritus, and the decomposing bodies everywhere. There are no signs of surviving humans, and I wonder, why me? The pandemic seized everyone by surprise. It was a colossal removal of human life without time to pray or say goodbye. The scene everywhere gives the impression that tornadoes struck everywhere, tossing vehicles like toys. The fires have consumed many buildings in every major city. Even now, after about ten years, the destruction of towns continues due to the wild blazes everywhere. I can only speculate about the sources for so many fires: people dying while cooking, candles left unattended, gas leaks, and many more causes too numerous to list. In particular the gas leaks are probably responsible for many explosions that leave buildings as if they were the result of bombings in a war. I have not found humans or animals anywhere. I wonder what happened to all the pets. Ants are multiplying, as well as other insects. I thought rats would be everywhere, devouring the corpses. The eating of contaminated corpses may have caused their extinction as well. My head is in turmoil, trying to make sense of this cataclysm in which I appear to be the only survivor. Then, there is the odor of decay and burned human flesh everywhere.

I have traveled on my motorcycle all over the country. I have entered many buildings and mansions. California provided me with a plethora of illustrations of how the wealthy and famous lived. I spent months and weeks in those places, yet I am always returning to the Quarter. The levels of perversion I could summarize from the sex toys and the contraptions I saw make me wonder if humanity was punished for all the depravity I discovered. The luxury in which a small portion of the nation's citizens dwelt was astonishing. I took a few items back to the Quarter with me, and I now wonder, what was the purpose of filling my building with all these items?

In most cases, these streets filled with crashed and burned vehicles posed so many questions. I read a fragment of Henry Miller (Tropic of Cancer) that I identify with under these circumstances: "My world of human beings has perished; I was utterly alone in the world, and for friends, I had the streets, and the streets spoke to me in that sad, bitter language compounded of human misery, yearning, regret, failure, wasted effort"—I can relate to the way he felt, although under different circumstances.

The question that keeps swirling in my brain is, why am I writing? What is the purpose of writing a novel no one will read? The couple of psychology classes I took at LSU led me to believe it is good therapy and what keeps me surviving. If I stop, I fear I will take the same measure some people in the Quarter did. I will continue writing for myself and determine how long I will resist the temptation of ending it all.

It should be noted I have been a loner all my life, and my friendship with Fred and during my attendance at LSU was one of the few periods during which I had an interaction with other humans. I am not taking into consideration those women who came to my apartment pursuing the pleasure of my tongue. I never cared for pets either, so my contact with Fred's cat was another exception to my life. To paraphrase Henry Miller, it is evident that I sometimes feel beneath my feet a hauling pit of emptiness. I continue writing because it gives value to the years I have left on this planet, even if there will be no one to read a line from it. I see the pandemic as a punishment for the chthonian mind of most humans.

I have been very fortunate that the Quarter has not had any fires. As often as possible, I search those buildings close to where I live to ensure there are no gas leaks or anything that will start a fire. Although some areas of N.O. have fallen prey to fires, I am pleased it has not been the case in the Quarter. I suspect the Quarter has become the omphalos of the world—perhaps of the USA. I guess the continuous drizzle has ameliorated the number of conflagrations from overwhelming the city. I revisited the Tulane library and found many interesting books I took to my building. I have one of the apartments dedicated to all the books I had brought from all over the USA—Harvard,

Yale, Princeton libraries, and many others. The apartment is now a library with fiction writers and poets I like, available for reading and citing. I also collected some psychology books that might explain why I have not succumbed psychologically to the pandemic.

I do not bathe every day and I limit myself to three or four days a week. I have gone to the relevant stores and liberated four bathtubs which I placed in the corner of Saint Ann and Bourbon to collect rain water. I then take bubble baths whenever I cleanse. I also have two large barrels collecting water for drinking. I never cared for alcohol so I empty the contents, and now have a large amount of water for drinking. My stash of cannabis has grown because that was one item I found frequently on my visits to hundreds of homes. The other drugs I found I did not touch because I fear an overdose—imagine, fearing death notwithstanding the condition in which I find myself!

Food has been easy to obtain with all cans that are lasting for decades. Since I am now a vegetarian, my dietary needs are very limited and, since I am not competing with anyone for food, I have not encountered any problems feeding myself. Thanks to my trips all over the nation, I have found countless cans of vegetables. I had no idea there were so many options! Actually, the barrels of rain water are not necessary since I have found plenty of bottles of spring water. Nevertheless, I keep those barrels bursting with rain water in case of any undesirable event that will keep me from roaming the country. I have several generators as well so I can power the two portable stoves where I prepare coffee and warm the food from the cans. At night I use gas lamps to read and move around the building. The result is that the generators have lasted me more than a decade. I also have boom boxes and several portable battery record players which make my life bearable with the plethora of records and cassette tapes. I have found all over the USA, popular, classical, and jazz music that I play whenever I can. I have some Bessie Smith, John Coltrane, Miles Davis, and the Beatles first pressing vinyl records that I found in the places I have visited—hundreds of record stores and private collections. I have obtained the addresses of many celebrities, actors, musicians to search their houses and have found a myriad of valuable items including vinyl records. I found some powerful shortwave radios, and every night I try to find a voice that will tell me I am not the only survivor.

I have continued my exercise routine with fifteen to twenty minutes of twenty-five pounds dumbbells and then I run around the Quarter for an hour. This also gives me the opportunity to detect any gas escaping or any fires in progress. As usual, there are no signs of life except for ants and other insects that are multiplying. I keep the ants at bay in the building with vinegar and pepper. I visited many hotels during my travels and found the bedbugs are augmenting. The first time in Hollywood, I went into a suite, pulled back the bedcovers, and found the white sheets were dark with lice and bedbugs. Just about every hotel was the same. The mansions, on the other hand, did not have that infestation yet.

Am I happy? I think I am. No humans around to respond and obey for my livelihood. Am I normal to feel like this? I was alone, and being alone I was free. From childhood I was independent. I did not need anyone for affection because I wanted to be free, free to do and to give only as my whims dictated. I always knew I was a misanthrope, but not to this extent. But I digress. I am planning to go to Mexico and Central America, but fear has been holding me back. Since I do not speak the language, I am concerned that my ignorance might create problems if I run into significant warnings. My plans to travel to many of those countries continue in my mind, nonetheless.

Why did so many people in the Q survived? Homosexuality cannot be the reason since I went to the "gay areas" of many cities and they were deserted—not one human around. I have found, however, many signs of suicide: hanging bodies, corpses holding guns, who knows how many people used other means to end their lives. Furthermore, I am not gay. It must be something else in the person's DNA. The incapacity to be alone which has led to the suicide of those who survive the pandemic makes me wonder about that flaw (?) in humans which demands relationships. Without such fellowships people are lost and the outcome is suicide. Who am I? What am I doing here? I never expected to have this absolute solitude. This is the kind of privacy many feared and drove them to suicide. And the silence everywhere is so loud that it too has propelled people into madness. I guess that the Q was not the only community that survived the pandemic, and after a few years, as happened here in the Q, they could not tolerate the post-pandemic environment and decided to leave this new mortal misery.

I have transformed the motorbikes to transport all the items I am bringing to my place. Tail bags, saddle bags, and other bags are now part of the several motorcycles I own. Unfortunately, Picasso, Miró, Warhol, and many other great painters, I could not carry on the bike. I found a small bust of Robert Kennedy at the White House that I keep on my desk where I am typing at this moment. I ask myself sometimes, would there have been a pandemic if RFK had not been assassinated? His involvement with civil rights was very important and the country's minorities owe RFK a great deal. I found some modern electric typewriters in several newspapers which I promptly liberated. I am employing one of them at this moment. I similarly have quite a collection of comic books. I now enjoy most numbers of my favorite, *Black Hawk*. My coin collection has grown substantially. Each of the apartments in the building are now dedicated to the different collections I am accumulating. All of these items and many more have made my life considerably pleasant.

The fog and the drizzle are everywhere in the country. In some places it is not as cold as in others. There is no snow anymore. I went to Chicago in December and there was the same drizzle and the temperature was in the lower sixties just as in San Francisco. In New Orleans it is around sixty-nine all year. Evidently, the weather on the planet has been affected as well. It appears that some animals are surviving and multiplying. The last time I took I-10 going west to Texas, in the area when one enters the Atchafalaya River and the swamp, I came upon a group of very large alligators that I had to shoot with my shotgun. Two of them were in my way menacing me and I had no choice. It was very unnerving because they were·so large and intimidating. Fortunately, my shotgun took care of them. It appears the earlier the animals were on the planet, their survival is assure--Ants, roaches, reptiles, and perhaps many others I have not seen yet. I am now wondering what creatures I might come upon on my travels. And since I was planning to travel to South America, the Darien area, among others, could definitely be very dangerous.

I have decided to stay home and spend time reading the books I have liberated from so many libraries and mansions. I am reading for a second time Henry Miller and his *Tropic* narratives. A younger version of myself was attracted to the books because they were prohibited, censored in the States. When one went through customs, copies of Miller's books were confiscated (James Joyce, as well) and that gave him a mystifying aura among the English specialists at LSU. A second reading of Miller's books, and after reading numerous authors, I realized that Miller shows no moral sense, no scruples, no shame in the portrayal of his characters. His novels also reflect the lack of honor of his protagonist, Henry. Henry also reflects the heartlessness of a jackal. Yet, what is more important, his works reflect the state of mind of the American society during those years. There are continuous shouts of antisemitism; the racism drips from the pages like blood from a wound; and more pervasive, the misogyny slaps one on the face as it appears in every page. Antisemitism, racism, and misogyny were present in the cinema as well. The *noir* films are an example of the misogynistic milieu of those years. Many other films, by the way, in which they portrayed black characters, reflected the acute racism affecting that period. The treatment of Jewish characters is subtle in films, but in literature it's much more open and obvious--particularly in Miller's novels. The hate for humankind those novels delivered, and the joy reflected by the narrator when he judges other characters negatively, reminds me of Meursault's speech at the end of *The Stranger* when he is waiting to be executed for the meaningless murder of a human being: "For everything to be consummated, for me to feel less alone, I had only to wish that there be a large crowd of spectators the day of my execution and that they greet me with cries of hate." Perhaps Mother Nature is punishing us for our behavior to each other and the way we have mistreated the planet.

I am starting to consider some ideas regarding the creation of this world that contemplates the possibility that this planet, as numerous others, were seeded by creators who were greater than us beyond description. They gave the opportunity to those seeded planets to develop and improve to their superior level. Some would be able to achieve such perfection. Others, unfortunately could not, due to a flaw during their development, and failure as a result. I fear we are in the latter category, and we are on our trail to extinction.

I found another story among Fred's maternal uncle's papers. As I mentioned before he was a teaching assistant when he was working on his doctoral at LSU. This is a short story that a student wrote during his creative writing class which he did not trash. It reminds me of how Fred lost his virginity with the family's housekeeper when he was a child. In the case of Fred, it was the housekeeper – whereas, in the story it takes place in a bordello at the hands of a prostitute – where the madame was the lover of one of his uncles.

THE DEBUT

It was Friday morning during a beautiful sunny day of spring with birds singing and butterflies dancing about. Geno was cutting school to make his first entrance into a brothel to lose his virginity.

Geno was unusually thin for his age. He would walk down the street with his head bent and his back arched—reminding one of a crooked paper straw. His clothes hung loosely from his body and danced along, moved by the breeze as if trying to escape. The most extraordinary thing about Geno was his eyes. A couple of big brown circles that protruded from his sockets and became part of the glasses he wore—giving the impression that he could have taken those spheres out as easily as he could his glasses. His mouth was always closed, but never straight. The lower lip permanently hung to the left, giving the impression that he was ready to smile from one moment to the next. Yet, this was never the occurrence. His hair was exceptionally black and never combed.

The home of Madame Claude (known as Lupa), was located on the central, old part of town (where the ancient mansions were), not quite in the shopping district, but close enough to observe people walking along with shopping bags with the names of the stores. Geno walked with his hands in his pockets, looking down as if seeking for pebbles to kick, while spitting on the pavement after every fourth or fifth strike. As he strolled along, he whistled one of Bach's fugues he played during his piano lessons. He looked around nervously hoping not to run into anyone he knew.

Once he reached Madame Claude's house, he wandered back and forth on the block where the mansion was located to assure himself that there were not any familiar faces around. He lit a cigarette, took a long drag to give himself courage, turned the lighted part into a pouch he made with his right hand, while holding it with his index and thumb. With this mode he could smoke in the street without taking the chance of someone scolding him. Out of habit, he walked into the lupanar with his hands in his pockets—a stream of smoke emanating from his right pocket as he walked up the steps to the entrance and rang the bell.

The door opened and an old maid (whose face was hidden by wrinkles) looked at him inquisitively. When she opened her mouth to ask what he wanted, her red, empty gums came into view:

"Watcha want Sonny?"
"Is, uh, Miss Claude in?"

"Yea…c'mon in"

In the living room the red walls were covered with erotic paintings—later Geno would discover that the entire house had erotic paintings hanging from the walls. Sitting on one of the stuffed couches in the living room was Lupa reading a book. Upon seeing Geno, she exclaimed:

"Hi! You are a Ripoll. Aren't you? I know a Ripoll when I see one. Your uncle Ralph and me had some wonderful salad days! He called me to tell me you were coming. I have a beautiful little thing for you. Is this your first time? She is only seventeen and hasn't been around long. You'll like her, honey."

The Ripoll name was well known around town. Geno's grandfather, Geno J. Ripoll, was a real estate mogul—he owned many office and apartment buildings. At school Geno received preferential treatment because his grandfather was a benefactor who had built several buildings for the school. However, Geno III, was also bright and absences from the school were readily excused and concealed.

Upon hearing the prospect of having a teenager as his first woman, Geno's lower lip dropped a bit further, and some of his white and perfect teeth began to appear briefly—not long enough to be considered a smile. He scanned the room for the right chair to sit down and upon doing so he felt the fullness of the velvety red and wide armchair. A soft drink was brought to him by a young scantily clad girl. As he drank the soda and Lupa continued the small talk, he scanned the room and saw a large painting which depicted a bacchanal in which a few young naked women catered to some old fat men. From where he sat, he could see a long hallway with several doors on each side. A young nude female sprang out from one of the closed doors as she was drying her face with a towel. She looked and smiled at him as she walked towards the end of the hallway. Her naked, plum derriere rocked from side to side like the pendulum of a grandfather clock. Geno followed her with his eyes, letting them caress every contour of her rose color generous buttocks. The boy swallowed the saliva accumulating in his mouth while he felt an erection beginning to surge. Gulping the saliva became extremely difficult since his throat had somehow knotted itself and there did not seem to be a way to disentangle it. Finally, the saliva emptied down his throat and Geno caressed his throat and noticed his hand was very cold. He drank the soda he discovered he was holding in his right hand and that helped calm him down. He started to wonder what he was doing there. His desire to experience sexual intercourse instead of masturbating had led him to ask his oldest uncle Ralph (a very cool guy) if he could suggest a means for him to have a woman. His uncle was greatly surprised, yet pleased. Geno's father had spoken to Ralph because he worried about Geno's lack of interest in girls. Geno was shocked. He simply found girls of his own age boring and untouchable because of the virginity commandment. Ralph told him the story of his relations with a prostitute, who was now a Madame, and how he and a group of friends met at her house a couple of times per month. I will arrange a date at her house for you, he said. He was there now, fearing the next move since his manhood was at stake. Nevertheless, he had to go through with the experience. This was another stage in life he wanted to have early—just as so many things in his fourteen years. He was a romantic slob, and he wanted to seize life in every possible way. During those classes at school that bored him – he considered irrelevant to the university – he would have Byron, Dumas, and other writers in the inside of the class textbook. Then he heard Lupa's voice telling him the girl was ready for him.

Geno forced his legs to lift his body out of the warm nest his thighs had made in the velvety chair. He got up slowly, feeling the blood rushing to his head and the burning sensation it created on his cheeks. He felt them warm and knew they were red. The awareness of his blushing made him blush further. His head began to whirl and his knees were petulantly refusing his commands. Finally, he managed to stagger down the hall towards a female who was standing by a door at the end of the hall. The hall had magically extended and would retrocede two steps for everyone he took. Eventually he found himself in front of the nude girl who would take his virginity. She greeted him with a kiss, and as he entered the room he was greeted with the scent of seashells—a marine whiff he had never inhaled before. She greeted him, and pointed to a chair where he could put his clothes. Geno looked around the room with green walls, and as the rest of the house, erotic paintings. There was a chiffonier in one corner of the room, allowing unseen space behind it. There was a night table at each side of the single bed. The bed was filled with stuffed animals and a rather large teddy bear was in the middle. She proceeded to remove them from the bed very slowly while giving Geno the opportunity to examine every curve of her body.

Her red nipples were gorged, and stood at attention waiting for her command as did the breasts from which they sprouted. Large and beautiful tan/bronze breasts that cried for attention and caressing. Her rosebush was two lines outlining her mount of Venus—like a volcano which erupted during her ejaculation—an experience Geno took with him the rest of his life. Geno stripped slowly and placed his clothes on a chair while she went to the bed and assumed the supine position. Geno followed her and began to suckle her nipples, and inserted his index finger in her pussy. There was some secretion there which surprised him since his uncle told him that he hoped she was a good performer because that always made the man feel extraordinary. He then concluded that she had creamed her pussy with some cream. The cream, he thought had a sweet aroma and trace of sea winds. She proceeded to hold his penis and brought him to her. He remembered that he was supposed to wear a condom and he got up took one out of his pants pocket and put it on. He tried to penetrate her, but he was too large, and with her eyes wide from admiration she said push. He did and she screamed from pain and pleasure.

After he put his clothes on, he took out his wallet and paid her; no longer looking at her beautiful nude body. Geno no longer noticing the beautiful breasts he had suckled, nor the way in which her belly molded as it met her mount of Venus: she had become another piece of furniture. Geno handed her the stipulated amount and when she took it, she went directly to the area behind the chiffonier. Curiosity overwhelmed Geno, and he followed her to discover there was enough space for her to enter and kneel before an old picture, faded by the years, of the Virgin Mary holding baby Jesus. Her lips were moving slowly as she prayed: "Dear Lady may this former virgin bring me a productive day."

The drizzle continues and the sun has disappeared from the sky. It is cold and humid and I wonder how many years have passed since the outbreak. I have not traveled much in the past year, but continue to find stories in the many boxes Fred saved in one of the empty apartments. I do not know if the following stories were written by Fred or by his maternal uncle. Perhaps they were written by the students in his creative writing class. The introduction to two stories are not signed, but it gives a general idea about the author. The stories are titled "The Potato Chip Kid" and "Chess Games." I am copying the introduction and the two stories.

INTRODUCTION

The following pages are attained from the journal of John Doucet, a convicted felon on death row of Louisiana's notorious Angola Prison. Since Mr. Doucet and I were good friends in the sixties, he asked me to find a publisher for his manuscript. Unfortunately, it is very difficult to find anyone interested in this type of material. Hence, I have decided to try publishing it a few excerpts at a time. I should like to stress the fact that the narrative here presented owes nothing to me except for its typing. The reader should also be aware that it is called a journal/diary in the sense that some of what is taking place in the narrative was written shortly after it took place. However, since there are parts which were rewritten several years later, as well as the addition of some passages, the term memoirs could be more appropriate. In conclusion, I believe Mr. Doucet has something important to say and perhaps the reader will agree with me.

July 1, 196_

THE POTATO CHIP KID

I got picked up by some weird chick after work today—10:00 p.m. to be exact. I remember the exact time because I was getting off work at that moment. I was working in those days at the Express Motel as a room clerk. It was not AAA approved and most people came in for a "quickie" so that the same rooms were rented several times in one night. I was crossing the street, getting ready to stick out my thumb to get transportation to the Quarter—that's what the natives of New Orleans called the French Quarter, which should really be called the Spanish Quarter due to its architecture—when a car stopped in front of me and a girl, roughly sixteen, chewing as she spoke, asked me where Elysian Fields Avenue was. Elysian Fields is one of the longest streets in New Orleans. It runs from the Mississippi River to Lake Pontchartrain, and it is a few blocks from the Quarter. I immediately suggested she allow me to show her the way and, surprisingly enough, she agreed. Before I got into the car my mouth began to water: after all, a sixteen-year-old chick, even if she speaks with her mouth full of food, is a good score at any time. I was twenty-five in those days: I had dropped out of college, had a lousy job, and a lot of rejection slips from hundreds of little magazines who did not like my stories. Consequently, such an opportunity to fulfill, to some extent, Nabokov's dreams, was not something to be discarded because of a mere mouthful of potato chips, as I was to discover later what she was eating. In the days in which this took place, teenage runaways were beginning to appear. It was not yet the everyday occurrence that it became a year or two later. Grass was still called pot and pin joints were smoked in closets. So, I was extremely moved by the possibility of having some young cunt that evening. As I sat next to her and she began to drive, I felt some very strong negative vibes: she talked away a mile a minute and stuck potato chips in her mouth between words. The shirt she wore had large pockets, and evidently she kept one bag of potato chips in each. I intuited she was a speed freak and began to get a little paranoid. After all, if she were stopped, I was in trouble: she was probably carrying all kinds of "shit" and the car could have been stolen. For a moment I was tempted to ask her to drop me off, but her skirt was raised far above her knees and they were plump and nice, "Ruben's thighs," I thought. Additionally, a sweet scent exuded from her—copulins secretions? I wondered. I talked myself into sticking around and checking her out a little longer before making any decisions.

The chick began to tell me about her crazy parents and how much she hated them: they lived in a small town somewhere in Alabama, the Chevy was hers and she was going to California. I suggested she spend the night in my pad where we could smoke some "Colombian Blue" and she could read some of my poetry—she seemed the type that would be impressed by the poetry bit. The pot was not really Colombian: it was home-grown—on an abandoned house's patio, in which some friends lived. My poetry was great, though the editors of Little Magazines didn't think so. She quickly agreed to spend the night, to my surprise, once again, and I began to feel my phallus rising. We were driving down Gentilli going west, and then we turned left on Elysian Fields going south, towards the river. Her conversation was limited to one topic, her parents. And her pockets were inexhaustible: potato chips sprouted out of them at the same speed words came out of her mouth—horns of plenty, both. Since she was driving a little too fast, I asked her to slow down. However, it was too late because out of nowhere came a motorcycle cop, and I began to think that my freedom was nearing its end. The kid, once again, to my surprise, was cool and composed. She came to a full stop, turned off the ignition, and turned on the interior lights. Then I discovered that although sixteen—I had asked her age earlier—she probably had been around longer than I. She raised her right foot (her gorgeous small toenails were painted red and looked like strawberries begging to be suckled), and placed it on the seat so that her white nylon panties could be seen even from where I was. The cop, no doubt, was going to have a better perspective. The move worked rather well together with her telling the cop she was from out of town: the cop spoke to her for about ten minutes or more, warning her about the need to stay within the posted speed limits and then let us go, without glancing at me once.

We got to the Quarter around eleven, and after circling my apartment several times, we finally found a place to park. When we got out of the car, I realized I had an erection quite noticeable in my tight jeans. I evoked then how as a boy, whenever an erection appeared, I could put my hands in my pockets and hide it from view—with tight jeans, it was not possible. But it didn't really matter anyway. In the Quarter people could go around naked and no one would notice them—except tourists.

We started to walk to my place and I began to shiver from excitement—like one feels when coming down from speed. She looked so good, so edible I was getting goosebumps: young and plump and so full of lust. My apartment was an efficiency on the corner of St. Ann and Bourbon—apartment one. I liked the number, and also the doorbell's location. Interestingly enough, it was at the bottom, so no one bothered me late at night. Not that it made much difference to me. I never went to sleep before 4:00 a.m.—which was about the time when everything began to slow down. There had been instances, though, fascinating ones, in which I had gone to sleep earlier than usual, and woke up with the impression that there were people in my room. Because my windows faced the street and I had no air conditioner, everything that took place in front of the windows drifted into the room. On some nights there were strange interludes between gay men. In one instance, I woke up as one party pleaded with the other to stop his running around. Other times the odor of weed would drift in, and I could almost get stoned from the fumes.

When the Kid and I went into my apartment, it was a quarter after eleven. My books were on the same board-and-brick shelves. My Picassos were still there—particularly the satyr with the large testicles which I had on the wall over the mattress on the floor, like a head-board. Modigliani's nude was still on the left wall above the tattered couch I had covered to hide its holes with an old, rat-bitten army blanket someone had left. I could see the bathtub's tiger paws showing through the crack in the old *biombo* that separated the room from the bathroom. She dropped her backpack and threw herself on the couch and said: "My name is Lily, what's yours?" I replied a la James Bond: "Doucet. John Doucet." "O.K. Johnnie, where's the dope. I am dying to try it out." I went outside, to the foyer, where I had my "stash" in a long and narrow closet which kept the electricity meters. The closet had a dirt floor where my weed was buried. I always wondered, particularly when I was stoned, if there were any "hot" wires under the soil—keeping the weed in my room was out of the question. The NOLA cops did not take the trouble of getting search warrants if they sniffed weed. I brought the "shit" to the room, rolled a couple of joints and we started to smoke while sitting on the mattress. When I started to feel good, I decided it was time for Walter Benton's *This Is My Beloved*, which usually does the trick. I asked her to read aloud to me a certain poem and she did, with a sense of cadence that surprised the hell out of me, once again:

Come home with me... that I may fill my arms with you.
Come where only I can see you, and undo your dress about your throat.
And my lips make the nipples of your breasts burst open

like acorns planted in warm spring soil. Come home with me...

After a few minutes of reading, she put the book down and started to take off her shirt. It seemed to be an army shirt dyed light blue. But the large pockets were an original addition. Under her shirt, as expected, was her youthful, bare, tanned skin. She was a redhead, yet she did not have the usual freckled skin one expects of redheads. Her skin was like milk mixed with a small amount of coffee. Her nipples were red, and rose from two small breasts which suggested a girl in her teens. Her tits were like two large scoops of vanilla ice cream with two cherries on top. She proceeded to take off her faded jeans and the sight of her mound of Venus with scattered red hairs barely covering it nearly made me have an orgasm. While she did her strip, she looked at me, smiling, teasing, knowing the volcano inside me was about ready to erupt. Then she lay down on the bed and spread her legs like a compass at a 150° angle—I almost had a premature orgasm. Playing "Mr. Cool," I slowly took off my clothes, and after folding them neatly (something I seldom do), put them on the only chair in the room. I suspected that this approach could increase her sexual appetite—a foreplay of sorts. Then we made love fast and furious and I wondered how it was possible that there were laws that might send me to jail for the rest of my life. She was as adept at fucking as I was. We spent most of the night copulating and in the morning, as I slept exhausted from all the action, she left. In the mirror of the bathroom she wrote with soap: "Thank you, Johnnie!" And the room was left with the scent of seashells for several days.

A week or so later, I began to notice a strange discharge from my penis. My fears were confirmed by a physician at New Orleans Charity Hospital and the penicillin he prescribed got rid of the gonorrhea. But somehow, after so many years, I will never forget the "Potato Chip Kid."

The adventures of John Doucet continue in the following quite violent story titled:

A GAME OF CHESS

My name is Doucet, John Doucet. The following is an excerpt from my journals which I have tried to glamorize somewhat by adding a few interesting embellishments to the events described, as well as creating some that only took place in my mind. The tone of my entire narration, as you probably have noticed already, is oral in the sense that the narrator is telling someone the events of that evening. I need to feel that I am telling you, the reader, directly those events that took place on a summer night of the year 1968 in the "Crescent City's" French Quarter. As I read my journals, I am reminded of many relevant issues—the social, political, literary, and artistic background of the times—which are independent from the incidents of the story, yet inseparable in my mind. I attended Warren Easton High School and it was my third year at Tulane when I was convicted and sent to Angola Prison for a crime I believe was justified—but that is another story yet to be told.

The entire anecdote takes place in a notorious tavern of the sixties where the Flower Children and the New Orleans Narcotics Unit hung out. The bar was located on Saint Phillip Street and it was called "The Seven Seas." The building's façade reminded me of Andalucia. The architecture in southern Spain and North Africa has whitewashed walls, large windows with iron grille-work, and high ceilings--which keeps them cool and airy in the summer. A sign several feet long protruded from the façade: a fascinating replica of a pirate ship carved out of cherry wood with the name "Seven Seas" in burnt green on the gunwales, above two tiny rows of cannons. The inside of the place has a large wooden bar extending on the west side of the room, made of wood left from a ship that had been the property of the owner, a retired merchant marine—or so he claimed. Behind the bar, most of the wall was covered by a mirror and on it a large sign written in green Gothic letters read: "Every night I put to sea in my dreams." Some of the benches, stools, tables, and odd decorations also came from the ship, including seven life preservers hanging on the walls with "Seven Seas" written in the same green lettering.

The present story has only one fully developed character, myself: narrator/protagonist. All the other characters are mere caricatures, unfinished projects who will appear for a moment or two, a few lines will briefly describe some personal attribute or flaw, and then they will disappear. Their physiognomy will be categorized as belonging to one of three groups: bird, muffin, or horse. Throughout your reading, you will find bracketed questions from my favorite books, a tattered amalgam of newspaper and magazine clippings, quotes from poems, bits of prose, etc.—in which I carry and read whenever possible. I most certainly hope that you will get to know me thoroughly; I want you to become a vampire of sorts, sucking away all my thoughts, my fears, my happiness, what have you. I do not plan to hold anything back; I want to tell you everything (let it all hang out, as we used to say); I will try to reconstruct it as it took place that summer night of 1968 at the "Seven Seas" in the Quarter.

To repeat myself, the "Seas" was the sort of place the "in" crowd frequented; the Beats were there before the Flower Children came along and adopted it. The interior of the "Seas" consisted of a very large room (formerly the living and dining room of the house) with two wooden columns raised midway, supporting an Arabic arch (horseshoe arch—the evil eye) which divided the room into two halves: the bar to the left as you came in, near the front door, and to the right were the tables and chairs; three chess tables where people played were against the wall across from the bar. Four bulky, hand-sawed wooden beams, bleached by age, extended from east to west perpendicular to the bar and the wall where the chess tables were located. They reminded me, when I was stoned, of dinosaur bones; other times I felt I was in the belly of a whale. From each beam hung several light bulbs dressed with multicolored red fringed lamp shades. These pseudo-Tiffany shades were found in many stores in the Quarter. The small light-bulbs immersed the room in perpetual twilight. The chess tables had their own lights that emanated from the wall where they were. Thus, the area where the chess tables were, was brighter (not much) than the rest of the place. The bar with its tall stools had a crowd of its own: the suds drinkers, students and tourists who came out of curiosity, and the older Quarter residents who knew the "Seas" had the cheapest beer in the area. The reddish-brown tables and tall-backed booths on the right side as you entered the space was the area where the flower crowd gathered. The four tables with chess boards had players and onlookers standing, some of them waiting to play, drinking coke and popping Dexies. The booths were occupied by trippers who came to listen to the music, buy, sell, score—all sorts of transactions took place in those booths. From the large room, you would go out to the patio and toilets, through a battered door on the north side of the house, opposite to the front door. The patio had tables and benches and a fountain with dead fish, insects, and beer cans. Smoking grass in the patio was overlooked by the management, but the narcs were usually sniffing around. Sometimes one could hear the warning "Hark, Hark, the Nark."

I would usually make the scene around 11:00 p.m. when tourists start to leave, and waited by one of the chess tables until I had my chance to play. Since I was a very good chess player, and most of the people who played were not, I played for hours until I was defeated or got tired. I was usually high on dexies, chewing gum, and drinking cokes.

["But I don't want to go among mad people," Alice remarked.

"Oh, you can't help that," said the Cat: "We're all mad here. I'm mad. You're mad."

"How do you know I'm mad?" said Alice.

"You must be," said the Cat, "or you wouldn't have come here."]

That particular night, I arrived at the Seas at my usual time and waited to play a fairly good player, a bird-faced character who was at that moment decimating the other player's pieces and leaving the board a bloody mess—I pictured it. I played this dude once before, and had a difficult time in defeating him. I should have played him immediately, as was the ritual in the Seas. I told him I was tired (true—I had been playing since midnight and it was 3:00 a.m.) when I checked the Mickey Mouse wall clock over the bar's mirror. But the truth was he was over thirty and not to be trusted. He was one of the best players around and, preceding our last and only encounter, he had been playing for several hours, defeating a number of opponents, until I check mated him. He had me cornered and was about to finish me off. Those watching began to whisper "Who is next? Who is next?" Suddenly, my bishop came from nowhere, it seemed, and mated him. He was tired, he was very eager to finish me off, in any case he did not see my Pawn opening the way for the Bishop. I got up and left; for I knew that if we played again, he would have crushed me. So, I knew he would be out for blood tonight. He had already defeated three opponents, I was told, severely, and I was witnessing the massacre of the fourth—obviously, I had a masochistic streak that evening.

Besides the chess games, the most fascinating experience, particularly on weekends when the crow was wall-to-wall, was to feel, see, smell (sperm, copulins, apocrines, gasoline, grass, tobacco), hear, even taste the people around the tables, pressing, leaning on the players. The Mickey Mouse clock over the large mirror hovering over the west wall usually indicated what sort of night it was going to be: some nights the hands would spin like tops, while other evenings, they seemed to be part of a slow-motion film.

["Life is no dream. Beware, beware!"
The beheaded sailor
Chanted on the water-bear
"Alleluia, Alleluia"]

The juke box was usually playing the week's favorites as well as the perennials groups: "The Beatles," "The Rolling Stones," "The Champs." Once-in a-while, teeny-boppers going through an exhibitionist streak would dance on top of the tables, wearing micro-skirts, often without underwear. While we played chess, to repeat myself, people would make a half moon to the players. I preferred the bench against the wall because I did not want distractions. While we played chess, people would stand very close around us, so close that one's shoulders and elbows frequently encountered soft flesh as well as fabric, and concentration was interrupted by their smells and conversations.

I finally sat down on the chair unprotected by the wall. He chose me from three who wanted to play him and I knew then he remembered me. He spoke immediately of our last encounter, and offered me the white pieces, notwithstanding the fact that white should have been his since I had not played the required game with him last time. It was clearly psychological warfare: he was establishing a continuation of our last meeting and he had nothing to fear from me. He had blonde hair and blue eyes. A privileged fuck, who probably never worked a day in his life, and an heir to many opportunities--smart enough to pick the best ones. He was wearing jeans with a tie dye designer t-shirt. I looked into his eyes and realized he was gay—I hadn't noticed last time! I am not gay, but I thought I had a sensor that is seldom wrong. Perhaps living in the Quarter for so long provided that ability, now I wonder. I take everything back that I thought about him, a few lines back. I am certain the dude has suffered a great deal. If he unmasked himself, his life at work could become what some young black men in financial institutions in New Orleans were going through. He looks like a banker or stock broker, perhaps? Our opening was quick:

	White	Black
1.	P-Q4	P-Q4
2.	N-KB3	P-QB4
3.	P-K3	N-QB3
4.	P-QN3	P-K3
5.	B-N2	N-B3
6.	QN-Q2	PxP
7.	PxP	B-Q3

In this manner I had the strong point of K5 and I had also opened the King file for my Rook. He then proceeded to B-Q3, and he castled and I followed at which point he slowed down, for he detected I had been reading up on chess and was better than last time. At this moment, perfume distracted my attention from the table to a figure practically resting on my right shoulder.

[But it was too late! The process taking place between
My eyes were revealing reality *in crudo*... it began by
Destroying salvation...]

She was a teeny-bopper with a thin flimsy fabric blue dress and it seemed she was not wearing any underwear because of the way the dress bonded with her breasts. The scent coming from her was a potpourri of grass, smegma, copulins, sperm, and sweat--I was fascinated by the blending. I could also detect the miscellany of odors coming from outside: Ripple and Midnight Express wines, perhaps coming from outside—homeless dwelt in the area. Many of the clients of The Seas preferred cheap reds: "Tokay's Okay!" The smell of fish also came through the main door that seldom closed, and created a draft with the patio door during windy and rainy nights. There was a fish-market the tavern would get a whiff of, if the wind was blowing through the right direction. Halitosis was a frequent smell of those flower children who believed that filthiness is next to godliness! The stench would strike my nostrils, and my stomach would summersault almost emptying itself onto the chess table. I was ready for situations like these: I'd take out my handkerchief, moistened with cologne, and would touch my nose with it, ameliorating the negative stench. I learned that trick from a Jesuit priest at the boys' school I attended. During confession, men usually kneel before the priest whereas women go to the tiny windows on the side of the confessional. The priest in question would place a handkerchief sprayed with cologne to keep halitosis and other smells from distracting him. My opponent moved to N-KR4, and I immediately realized he was planning to move to B5 next, so I moved to P-N3 while wallowing in the sweet scent of cannabis permeating the place—you could almost get stoned from the fumes. Then I heard the lyrics from one of my favorite songs screaming out of the juke box a few feet away: "I love you baby and if it's all right I need you baby..."

I turned to get a look at the girl on my left, and inhaled an overwhelming stench of decaying sea-shells which emanated from her écu that was almost to the level of my nose. [Noli me tangere.] She did not appear to be older than sixteen, which was typical Saturday nights when the fake identifications and the bouncer's kindness allowed people younger than eighteen to enter the place. I looked up, she was grinning and her dress clung to her plumpness, allowing for a full appreciation of her youth. Although it was a bit dark where she was standing, it was not difficult to appreciate her pubic triangle and her large nipples. She was fair-skinned with short blonde hair. I could visualize her nude: her large breast and her blonde hair covering her mount of Venus. My opponent moved to P-B4 and I decided to concentrate on the game and forget temptation—she was no doubt a tease. We had no time rules during the games and there was no clock. One could get up and walk around between moves if one so desired. I moved my knight to K-5 and got up to go to the head. The lyrics "Love, love, love" followed me through the door into the patio and to the bathroom's doors.

[Yeah, man, anything you say, of course. Whatever
Your drug is that's your pleasure, whatever your
Love is that's your love.]

I had a lot of difficulty navigating to the bathroom since the place was unusually crowded. I suspected the tavern was beyond the capacity of people the fire department advised. I had to wait for the dudes who were waiting in line. Fortunately, I did not have a dire need. The men's room was barely bigger than two closets—just enough space for a toilet and a basin with a broken, cloudy mirror hanging precariously from the wall. The whitewashed walls were covered with graffiti: "Frodo lives;" "Jesus is God's atom bomb;" "Folk you;" "Nirvana needed (a cannabis leaf drawn);" "Charybdis sucks;" and many homosexual propositions with dates and hours. There was also the restroom poetry: "Here I sit broken-hearted/ came to shit/but only farted."

[I'm obsessed with *Time Magazine*, I read it every week,
… It's always telling me about responsibility.
Businessmen are serious. Movie producers are serious.
Everybody is serious but me!]

I left the head and went to the bar, one of the bartenders "Little Joe," was rushing around doing his thing. Little Joe was a speed freak and you could see the meth in his eyes if he took off his shades—a rather unusual event. His long brown hair came down to his shoulders and he had a Zapata moustache on his muffin face. Since he was about 5'2", he wore cowboy boots with several inch heels. The most interesting feature about him was the beautiful blue suede pouch hanging from his wide black leather belt which bounced with every movement he made. For some, he was even more interesting to watch than the other bartender: a 5'10" amazon and definite horse face wering a leopard-spotted bikini and went by the name of "Sheena of the Jungle." Sheena kept the tourists and booze-heads glued to their stools when not on their toes, for she was frequently bending down picking cherries. And sometimes she would climb on the bar to dance to the rhythm of her favorite tunes. This night she was dancing to "The Letter" that had her going (and who knows what drug she was taking) as I watched while sipping a coke I got from "Little Joe" and walked back to the chess table where my opponent had moved his knight to B3. The teeny-bopper was sitting in my chair, with her skirt spread out and her vulva touching the wooden chair. She got up quickly when she saw me, and as I sat down I touched the chair surreptitiously to feel her warmth and the moisture left by her pussy. Again, I forced myself to concentrate on the game and moved my Pawn to KB4, and in so doing he took my knight with his Bishop. I furtively brought my hand to my nose and I could smell the fish scent of her snatch. I began to wonder if I should forget the game and try to make it with the chick when a paranoid inspiration hit me: Could she be a decoy planted there to distract me and not pay attention to the game?

[. . . group solidarity is necessary before a group can operate effectively from a bargaining position of strength in a pluralistic society. Traditionally, each new ethnic group in this society has found the route to social and political viability through the organization of its own institutions...

Studies in voting behavior specifically, and political behavior generally, have made it clear that politically the American pot has not melted. Italians vote Rubino over O'Brien; Irish for Murphy over Goldberg, etc. This phenomenon may seem distasteful to some, but it has been and remains today a central fact of the American political system.]

I took his bishop with my BP and he moved N-K5 fearing my deadly pawn. I decided to move my Queen to K2 and threaten his knight. He responded by moving his Queen to N3. I started to scribble on my notepad his move, as well as some interesting conversation I have been listening to around me. (I failed to mention that one of my many habits is carrying a notebook wherever I go and in high school I took typing and short hand for moments like this). Then, suddenly, it hit me in the face with such force that I gasped and dropped my pen. Obviously, someone had been to "Buster Holmes" and had too much of the 50-cent special: red beans and rice with a slice of French bread. The stench was overpowering: silent but deadly. Springing up, I took my handkerchief out of my pocket and brought it to my nose and rushed to the bar to ask Little Joe for an incense cone (free on demand). Sheena had stopped dancing on top of the bar and was in the process of straightening her bikini top. She usually behaved this way when there were businessmen around that could provide her with some extra cash. Sheena wasn't a professional prostitute, but she did a trick or two occasionally when she liked the man and the price was right. She used to say that people should examine the merchandise before buying, and after a few minutes of heavy dancing she would straighten her bikini in front of the large mirror, taking the top off enough to expose most of her large breasts with their pointed nipples, and then moving the lower part to show some of her pubic bush. I had grown accustomed to her antics and didn't look at her for too long, but focused instead on the two businessmen she was getting ready to hook.

["We wanted exactly what happened. We wanted the tear gas
to get so heavy that reality was tear gas. We wanted to create
We wanted to create a situation in which the Chicago police
And the Daley administration and the federal government and
The United States would self-destruct. We wanted to show that
America wasn't a democracy, that the convention wasn't politics.
The message of the week was of an America ruled by force. That
was a big victory."]

They were too old to be trusted, late forties perhaps, and obviously had recently removed their convention badges to paint the town. I felt sorry for their wives because, if the Johns were not careful, they would be taking home a good dose of clap. Sheena often mentioned, during nights when the place was almost deserted and the regulars sat at the bar to shoot the breeze, her visits to a physician in the Quarter who gave penicillin without asking questions. Little Joe gave me incense and I went back to the table. Everyone in the vicinity of the table had moved away amidst guffaws, clapping, shouting, and cursing. My opponent was returning with a beer, and I carefully stood the incense cone on top of my empty coke can.

The table and chairs were pinkish-red cedar and the chess board was part of the table top. The chess pieces, the coke can, the incense cone with the spiraling smoke had a surrealistic look about it—better yet, it had a Warholish appearance as I stood looking down. The table also had a mosaic of graffiti ("SDS will overcome," "SNCC," Drop Out") that gave the table a consciousness of history, of age, as if it were a veteran with the scars of forgotten encounters. I was particularly fond of its smell: the coats of paint, varnish, glue, and nails had not erased the scent of the sea. I was listening to the surf in a sea-shell whenever I smell the furniture of the "Seas." We sat down quickly, both wanting to finish the game, which had been going on for nearly an hour. It was past 1:00 a.m. and we started almost at midnight. We had moved our Queens and it was my turn to do something decisive. The crowd had gathered around us again and I was becoming impatient. Whenever such a thing happens, I would start to rock back and forth on the chair, lifting the front legs and putting all my weight on the rear ones. I decided my knights were going to take the lead and moved to B3. While I waited for his move, I heard whispers over my left shoulder, something about a couple of bombs going off at the New Orleans Custom House. It was brief and to the point: "Where?" "Custom House--The ashtrays on the side doors--Timed after closing. Very small, just big enough to make a lot of noise and shatter some glass windows." "Okay, I'll pass the word." "See you there in a couple of hours." "Power to the people." I looked up and did not recognize them. Obviously, the Weathermen were operating in New Orleans. I made a mental note to stay away from the corner of Canal and Decatur. My opponent moved his Bishop to Q2, clearly in-order-to bring together the Rooks, since he was limited by his own Knight and Pawns blocking the movement. I decided to counter the possibility of attack on my Queen's side as he has so much artillery concentrated there: Queen, Knight and Bishop, if he moved his Knight out of the Bishop's path. I moved my Pawn to QR3 and he responded quickly, moving his King to R1.

[An apron full of chopped fingers]

At that moment, there was a commotion at the entrance: the front door was slammed hard and a hoarse voice boomed: "DON'T NOBODY MOVE OR I WILL BLOW YOU SKY HIGH! DO YOU HEAR ME, MOTHER FUCKERS? TURN OFF THAT FUCKING JUKE BOX FAST" I froze with only the chair's two rear legs touching the worn Andalusian tiling I had so often admired, wishing I could lay there at this moment out of harm's way. I could barely see him with a side glance as two of them were moving toward the patio, I assumed. They wore stockings over their heads and carried sawed-off shotguns. They locked the door and put up the Close sign, while they were ordering everyone to move to the North area of the room. Only one of them was talking: "Take it easy, do what you're told and no one will get hurt. My partners are bringing in the customers from the patio and restrooms. (There were several masked men with shotguns and there was nothing we could do.) I want you to get ready to deposit all your valuables in the bags as they circulate among you. Don't nobody move until you are told." I was beginning to come down from the Dexies, stopped chewing gum, and the trembling associated with the withdrawal from the drug began to hit me. A cold chill came over me and I could not stop trembling. I had my fingers barely holding on to the table, and I did not want to get the chairs' four legs on the ground fearing the man with the shotgun would fire because I was moving. The main guy, the one who did all the talking decided to provide some entertainment while his partners did the rounds collecting valuables. He ordered Sheena and one of the business men to take off their clothes and dance on top of the bar. His partners behaved as if they had all the time in the world making small conversation with their victims as they went along seizing valuables and making everyone take their clothes off. They were taking advantage of the women's nudity by pinching their nipples, slapping their buttocks, and uttering obscenities. There was only one public phone in the place, and no way we could contact the police. The two on the counter were nude and the businessman was obviously not in the mood. The whole tableau was grotesque: an excellent example of gallows humor. The boss became more sadistic and started poking the businessman in the rear with the gun barrel. As he did, I noticed the copper bracelet he was wearing on his right wrist and notwithstanding the silk stocking over his head I recognized him: a well-known speed freak with arms like road maps, now covered with a long sleeve shirt, who would go on sadistic binges, hunting stray dogs and cats that he would skin alive. The situation at the "Seas" suddenly appeared more serious, and my shivering increased so much that I lost my balance and fell backwards with a crash. The speed freak, who had been poking the businessman was so startled that he whirled and fired in our direction without looking. The teeny bopper received the full blast and fell on me: brains, bones and blood were smeared on top of me. The gorgeous young female was now a bloody trembling, jerking mass, dead yet her body was still moving, refusing the arrival of death, wriggling like a beheaded chicken. I was under her body, hearing shotgun blasts and struggling to get out from under her since I could see people running toward the exit doors. Pandemonium was gripping the "Seas" and I could not move her from enwrapping me. The *Times Picayune* gave details the next morning of the evening events. The people had overcome two of the invaders and Little Joe shot the boss and another thieve who was in the process of emptying the cash register.

[The three greatest tumults of the world—the Deluge, the Crucifixion,
The Day of Judgment—near at hand.]

Finally, I managed to push her body off me, bolted for the door and out into the rain (another New Orleans summer shower) trying to remove, as I ran, blood, brains, and teeth.

I returned yesterday morning after spending several weeks in Florida and Georgia rummaging thru some beautiful mansions—very fast, I must say—because I saw signs of cruelty. In Tampa Bay, in one of the mansions, I found a man shot in the head. He had the book he was reading still in his hand: *The Selected works of Philip K Dick*. I decided to take it with me and abandon the area as quickly as possible. There was the word "Christians," written in blood in several places. The drizzle in many coastal areas is causing flooding, and in those zones it is no longer possible to drive because the streets are underwater. In addition, the beaches are now under water. Highway 98 that parallels the ocean in Mississippi is now under water and I had to get my bike on Interstate 10 going to Atlanta and returning from Tampa. I found a collection of *Black Hawk* and *Superman* comic books in Miami Beach to add to my collection. When I got back to the Quarter yesterday, I found three dismembered bodies at the entrance of Royal and Esplanade. The U-Haul truck was blown up and the three bodies strewn around. I am glad there are three seniors now living in the Quarter. They appeared individually and unexpectedly not long ago. They left the bodies around the entrance with the expectation it will be a deterrent to other marauders. I knew the three men left in the Quarter had checked every house—since we have a marker on the doors that indicate someone's entrance. The three Quarterites left (Jack, Pierre, and Julian) came to see me, as usual after long trips, to ask me to tell them what I saw and found. I always provide them with food, accounts about the environment and other items that might benefit them--books, in particular. They in turn would inform me of the events that took place while I was gone. They assured me that everything was under control. I notify them that there are survivors in other cities and they seemed to be sadistic. They were white fascists and used Christianity as a rationalization for what they were doing. In Florida I found a white flag with a black swastika—the corpses by the Royal entrance seemed not to have any flags. However, two blocks away from the incident there was an unknown yellow pick-up truck that had some Christian literature and a copy of Hitler's Biography. We assumed it belonged to the corpses and concluded the Christians were in New Orleans. We discussed and made plans for the possibility of other unwelcomed visits and after a long conversation, it was decided to leave the bodies as they were at the entrance to Royal. Jack would rig the trucks with dynamite again. Jack was a World War II veteran who was a whiz with explosives and had rigged all the entrances that way. The only entrance without explosives was Bourbon and Esplanade. The three musketeers, who were not inclined to leave the Quarter, needed more food so I decided to go to the only Schwegmann's I hadn't visited on 5300 Gentilly Road. I had started a vegetable patch in St. Louis cemetery with cantaloupe, eggplant, collards, cucuzzi, okra, sweet potato, but it is not doing well. It was the best plot of land I could find close to my place and it was in a cemetery! I was hoping as well to give the three men an occupation since they had so little to do except read. I will keep looking for some other area close to the Quarter since the three guys did not want to go too far away from their homes. We were living very close to each other in the houses located on Bourbon and Saint Ann. At night they would take turns to keep watch of the entrance on Bourbon and Esplanade. Since they did not go out, I would go to the grocery stores every week, and when I left for a long period, upon returning, I would go out again replenishing supplies. Since I was out for several weeks the supplies had diminished quite a bit, I decided to take the pick-up truck that the Christians had brought to Esplanade. I could load a large amount of supplies in it. The problem with the myriad of vehicles on the streets we had partially resolved years earlier so there would not be a problem driving the large truck on the streets. The number of people who were in the Quarter post-pandemic were not originally from there, some of them came from the outside looking for friends and relatives and decided to stay. Most of them passed away by their own hand or left hoping to find relatives in other cities.

The three men left in the Quarter had had very interesting lives. Jack Pottier was a World War II veteran who enlisted after finishing high school. He fought in the Battle of the Bulge where he suffered a leg injury that left him with a limp. He married and had children and grandchildren who perished during the pandemic. His wife owned a house in the Quarter inherited from her father and that is how Jack came to live in the Quarter. His war stories kept us entertained at night while we drank wine and smoked pot. Jack was a nocturnal person who spent his nights on the roof of Bourbon Orleans, where he could keep an eye on the entrances that were not booby-trapped with explosives: Canal and Esplanade. He had been a sniper in WWII and continued to be a master of the rifle. He killed two individuals who tried to enter the Quarter one night. He slept most of the day, and at night he kept awake with coffee and a short-wave radio, where he sometimes heard foreign languages he did not understand, but hearing voices was enough to keep him hopeful and awake.

Julian Boudreau was a gay man and manager/part owner of the Bourbon Orleans Hotel. The hotel occupied a block on Orleans, Bourbon, St. Ann, and Royal streets. He was a gay man very well connected with the upper classes in the Crescent City. He provided many well-connected men (politicians, wealthy and upper class) some special suites where they could have their liaisons without fear. He also told stories about the women those men brought surreptitiously to his hotel.

Pierre Leblanc worked as a stockbroker in New York, and retired early after working about seventy hours a week for most of the twenty-five years as a broker. He accumulated a couple of million before he retired, and his plan was to travel all over the world. He was on vacation in New Orleans when the pandemic emerged. He had been married several times and never had any children.

I am not sure how many years have passed since the advent of the pandemic. Perhaps thirteen, fifteen years, I have lost count. The drizzle continues and the sun is hidden behind huge dark clouds, while I drove to the Schwegmann in Gentilly. I was armed with a Thompson submachine gun— "Chicago typewriter"—a blowback-operated, selective-fire submachine gun, invented by the

United States Army brigadier general, John T. Thompson, in 1918. I also carried a Smith & Wesson Model 29. It was heavenly that there was a police station in the Quarter (334 Royal Street, to be precise) where we have a myriad of weapons and motorcycles available to us.

As soon as I arrived to the store, I covered my face with a surgical mask because the corpses, the rotten meat from the butcher shop and many other decaying items gave the store a stench that was very difficult to overcome without a mask. A cold wind was sifting the fine rain as I went out into the deserted street. While I was driving, I could hear the drops with a rhythmic patter hitting the truck's windshield. Shampoo and soap were among the items I had to find in the store. We were now taking a bath where the JAX Beer building is located. The water from the Mississippi has overtaken the lower area of the building and was about to overwhelm the river levee and inundate Decatur Street. To some extent that was fortunate since people could have entered the Quarter by way of the river levee. As I drove to the store, I reflected on how fortunate we were that only one helicopter had crashed in New Orleans at Lake Pontchartrain. During my travels I had seen a myriad of crashed planes with subsequent massive fires. I arrived at the store and was awfully surprised to find very few corpses and the shelves were relatively untouched. I took several shopping cart trips to the truck with mostly canned food (I practically took everything that was left), saltine crackers, Wasa crispbread, bottled water, wine, beer, and any food that appeared unspoiled. Since the back of the pick-up was full, I was doing the last trip with the shopping cart and happy to have found so much. Suddenly, I heard a female voice behind me saying: "Hands up, Christian." I raised my hands and replied: "I stopped believing when I graduated from Jesuit High and no longer was forced to go to mass on Sundays." "Turn around with your hands up." I did so and almost gasped to find this young woman (eighteen, nineteen?) with a machine gun pointing at me. She was big (5'9", 5'10'? taller than me), lanky and velvety. She had a feline characteristic about her: with that silky, deceptive strength of feline species—the crouch, the spring, the pounce. She had curly red hair and lips that seemed to have been sculpted from an African-American female. Her buttocks too, suggested African heritage, as I was to determine later. Mia Concepción was her name and, without realizing it, she extracted the outmost delight from the senses she had been endowed with, and from her particular figure, her color, her hair, her voice, her skin, her temperament, and not realizing how people, not just men, reacted to her. We talk for a while and she asked several questions and my answers confirmed that I did not belong to the insane sect. She knew that the yellow pick-up I was driving was used by them, so she assumed I was one of the Christians. She agreed to go to the Quarter and we got into the truck to drive there. As we were on our way, I detected her strong scent. From under her arms, I scented shallots, and her pussy, her rose bush, had the aroma of copulins, of seashells. My impaired penis wanted to get an erection and the tiny entity between my legs felt rigid.

After I told her a bit about the people in the Quarter of which only three were left, she asked how it was possible for so many people to have survived whereas in the rest of the USA perhaps only about two in a million had survived. She had driven to the West and found no one. I then explained that most of those fifty were survivors in the hotels who came from all over the world. Some of them left to look for their families and never came back. When we arrived to my destination, I drove several times around the Quarter examining all the entrances and surrounding areas without noticing anything amiss. I entered through the Bourbon and Esplanade entrance and the guys were waiting impatiently for me fearing the Christians had captured or killed me. They were very surprised to see Mia with me and they called for a celebration. I suggested we all take a bath and Mia could do it first out of our sight in one of the tubs and we would go afterwards.

After the bath we went to the Bourbon Orleans ballroom to eat and celebrate the appearance of Mia, and it was a good opportunity for her to tell us about her adventures and background. She told us how she was kidnapped by the Christians in a grocery store when she was twelve and witnessed their eating the flesh of a person they captured—she refused by telling them she was vegetarian. Their belief was that the Bible spoke of eating human flesh; and therefore, it was the right thing to do during these brutal times. She was instructed on the use of guns, driving, the Bible, cooking, and a few other skills for survival. However, when her parents died, she had already been schooled in survival skills by her father. The morning the pandemic broke she woke up and was surprised her parents were not up. Needless to say, she was traumatized to find them dead in bed. She spent over two years in the bunker before she ventured out on her bike to search for groceries when she was seized by the Christians. After a year with the Christians, she escaped and dedicated herself to hunt them, and killed about twenty of twenty-five who were part of the group. She was handy with the rifle and was able to find elevated places where she shot them. There were only five women among the group of christians who were trying to conceive: all of them aborted their fetuses after five months. It seems those women who survived were prevented from having children by the virus existing in their system. According to Mia, the three bodies that came in the yellow Ford pick-up were not local Christians, even though the vehicle had a Louisiana license plate. They had come from another colony a few years back. It was decided we had to be more vigilant, and would begin a night patrol to prevent unexpected surprises since Jack was only monitoring the Bourbon entrances. Mia lived in a mansion in Audubon Place on St. Charles Avenue in a private enclave of some of the wealthiest people in New Orleans. Her parents had Ph.D's from the University of Florida where they met and fell in love. Her father was of Irish descent and had inherited money from his father—Mia's paternal grandfather. On her mother's side, they were exiled Cubans who came into the country legally and with enough money to start a restaurant and eventually they developed a well-known restaurant chain in Florida. Her maternal grandmother was a Cuban octoroon and I detected her black ancestry when I saw her for the first time.

Mia's father, John, has a stirring history in Florida and was the motivation for his constructing a very thorough basement in their house. When he was around nine, a class five tornado shredded their house in Florida and killed his father. Her mother, Ester, did not work and had the financial means to move immediately to Columbus, Georgia to stay away from hurricanes and tornadoes. John decided, when it was time to select a university, to go to the University of Florida where he met Mia's mother. The first years of marriage were difficult because it was problematic to find work at the same university. Furthermore, Ester had a problem conceiving, which was very disappointing to them since they wanted a child before she began teaching. Finally, they received an offer from Tulane which they accepted immediately. Ester would be teaching Spanish and French literatures and John would be teaching Biology. Ester had several miscarriages before Mia was conceived and the child became a difficult pregnancy. After Mia's birth, Ester was informed she could not have any more children. Mia was an exceptional child and later, when she took an IQ test, it was discovered she had an IQ over 140. She started attending Ursuline Academy, one of the most distinguished girls' Catholic schools in N.O. By the time the pandemic appeared she was in 10th grade and, after school, Monday through Thursday she had a tutor for an hour on different subjects not covered very deeply in school. Mia had tutors for Greek, Latin, French and Spanish literatures, History, and piano lessons. All of these, plus reading books she found cited in her readings and lists provided by her tutors, contributed to her knowing enough to become a sophomore in college. It should be noted, however, that the sciences had been neglected except for what she took at school.

Two days later she took me to her home and I appreciated much better John's paranoia which provided her daughter's survival. In the two nights she spent in one of the apartments in my building, she discovered the myriad of books I had liberated from all over America and she asked me for several she had not read. Mia's father, John, as a result of his traumatic experience in Florida, built a basement – more of a bunker – under their palatial house. The floor of a utility room in the kitchen could be lifted and some stairs led to a large room that was almost as big as the first floor of the house (which had three floors). The South and East wall were covered with shelves filled with cans of food and different provisions that could probably last a family of three for a couple of years. There were a couple of generators and a large refrigerator and a freezer that was also filled with foodstuff when there was electricity. There were shelves filled with guns and rifles and on the Northwest wall was a paper shooting target for practice. On the Northeast side were two adult bunkbeds and a little round table with three chairs. The entire place was soundproof, as a result of its concrete construction with noise absorbing wall panels, which did not allow any noise to penetrate nor get out. The ceiling was padded with some sort of thick white squares (acoustic ceiling clouds) that also contributed to its soundproofing. There were two exercise machines (a treadmill and a stationary bicycle) and some dumbbells which would allow anyone to keep herself in very good shape. She spent over two years in the basement without going anywhere. When the food started to decrease, about two years later, she ventured out and was kidnapped by the Christians. During the two years she was in the bunker she read all the books her tutors had suggested. They gave her lists on the different areas which she brought and did not have time to read before the

Pandemic emerged. He also went through her parents' libraries so that she was well instructed in science because of her father's books.

Mia was with the Christians for about a year where she was trained with firearms and how to be a good wife and mother. There were about twenty males and five females who would get pregnant and would spontaneously abort after four months. She was thirteen when they captured her, and she played along until she had the opportunity to escape. I suspect the fact that she was catholic helped Mia a great deal and she was being groomed for better things, according to one of the Christians, who was the leader of the group in the area. Mia realized that she had to escape from the group and she did as soon as they were separated one night when all the men went out and the women remained behind. She returned to her house and took a sniper rifle with a silencer, and began her extermination of the sect. According to Mia, she killed twenty at different times since she knew their movements, it was easy to find tall houses and trees. The silencer kept them from detecting where the rounds were coming from. She usually took out one at a time to keep them from detecting her. One of Mia's favorite quotations from the Bible was:

The heathen are sunk down in the pit that they
Made: in the net which they hid is their own foot
Taken. The Lord is known by the judgment which he
Executeth: the wicked is snared in the work of his own
Hands. The wicked shall be turned into hell.

I found more items that interested me among Fred's uncle's papers. It appears that he found some of the carbon paper transfer sheets of the courtroom scribe of a very important trial in New Orleans. James Garrison, the District Attorney of Orleans Parrish, began an investigation of the assassination of JFK and the prosecution of New Orleans business man Clay Shaw. The carbons describe among other items the Zapruder film and the presence of Badge Man in the grassy knoll.

Here are some examples of the trial:

Q   Would you indicate to the Gentlemen of the Jury by stepping to this aerial photograph the route taking by the presidential limousine?

A   The limousine was going west on Elm, north on Houston and back west—pardon me, west on Elm, north on Houston and back west on Elm.

Q   Mr. West, is it possible for you to tell the Gentlemen of the Jury the approximate span of the time that elapsed between the first report which you heard and the last report which you heard?

A   No, sir.

Q   Mr. West, when was the last time you observed the presidential limousine?

A   Somewhere shortly before it went under the triple underpass.

Q   Were there many persons in Dealey Plaza …

The questioning about the Dealey Plaza restart and Mr. West is asked how long has he resided there:

A   Oh, since 1942.

Q   Is it not a fact, Mr. West, that Elm Street, before it goes under the triple overpass, declines rather sharply?

A   Considerably.

Q   Is it not also a fact, Mr. West, there being many buildings around Dealey Plaza there, that you have the effect of a valley which is very susceptible to echoes and in which it is very difficult to determine the direction from which sound is coming?

A   Number one, I don't remember ever having heard an echo, or what I knew was an echo. As to which way sound is coming from, I don't know I ever had any trouble.

Q   You say you heard four noises, the first two of which you thought were motorcycle backfires and the last two of which you thought were sots, is that right?

A   Right.

Q   Mr. West, in your mind are your[sic] positive as to the number of sounds you heard, or is that a matter of some conjecture?

A   That was my response on that day.

Q   You do admit, sir, the circumstances were very exciting and created a situation which was very possibly susceptible to error, do you not, sir?

A   They were extremely exciting.

Q   I take it you recognize the fact you could be mistaken as to the number of sounds, is that right, sir?

A   It is possible.

Q   Mr. West, do you remember approximately when the parade route, that is the route which the presidential motorcade would take, was made public in Dallas?

A   No, sir, I do not.

Q   Could you tell us approximately how long before the 22nd of November, 1963—

Mr. ALCOCK:
        Objection, he has already answered the question.

THE COURT:

> I will sustain the objection. If a person says he doesn't know how can

[page missing]

> in Fort Worth that the plans were for him to come to Dallas.

Q   Did you know as much as a week before November 22?

A   I couldn't say.

Q   Mr. West, would you mind stepping down to this plat here and pointing out the relative positions—

THE COURT:

> Your back is turned to the Court Reporter, Mr. Dymond, so would you mind speaking loudly, please.

By Mr. Dymond:

Q   The exhibit is State-35. Would you point out the relative positions where you were standing and the spot where you saw the motorcade first on Elm Street? Would you put your finger on each one of them?

A   I was standing at the point indicated by the pin here at the southeast corner of the intersection of Main and Houston. The first time I saw the motorcade at Elm Street was at this point here immediately after we have turned onto Elm Street.

Q   Would you kindly place an X on the spot where

[Several pages missing]

Q   Is it not a fact, Sir, some of the actual participants in that motorcade ran back towards the grassy knoll area after the shots were fired?

A   I don't know who they were. I know the city policeman whose motorcycle was parked there at the curb was up on the grassy knoll.

Q   I take it you don't know if they were trying to get away from the shots or why they were going over the fence?

A   No, sir.

MR. RAYMOND:

> That's all, thank you, sir.

REDIRECT EXAMINATION

BY MR. SCIAMBRA:

Q   Mr. West you went in the direction of the grassy knoll—

MR. DYMOND:

> Objection to leading the witness.

MR. SCIAMBRA:

> He testified to it.

MR. DYMOND:

> I object to repeating the witness' answer.

[PAGE MISSING]

…what direction would you go on reaching Houston?

A   I would go to Elm Street.
Q   Why is that, sir?
A   To get into the Stemmons Freeway.
Q   Why would you turn off of Main Street at that point?
A   There is no access from Main Street to the Stemmons Freeway. The only access to it is from Elm Street.
Q   Did you testify before the Warren Commission?
A   No, sir.
Q   Did any FBI agent ever interview you?
A   Ever What?
Q   Ever interview you relative to what you heard in Dealey Plaza.
A   No, sir.

MR. SCIAMBRA:

> I have no further questions.

RE-CROSS-EXAMINATION BY MR. DYMOND:

Q   Did you ever see Lee Harvey Oswald there?

A   No.

Q   Did you ever see this Defendant, Clay Shaw there?

A   No, sir.

[SEVERAL PAGES MISSING]

Q   Thank you. Have your seat back, please, on the stand. Mr. Zapruder, as you were standing in this location that you have pointed out taking your motion pictures what, if anything, did you see as you took this film? Would you please describe it for the Jury?

A   I don't understand the question.

Q   What did you see as you took your films in Dealey Plaza that day? Explain to the Jury.

A   I saw the approaching motorcade of the President coming from Houston Street, turning left on Elm Street and coming down towards the underpass. As they were approaching where I was standing, I heard a shot and noticed where the president leaned towards Jackie. Then I heard another shot which hit him right in the head, over here, and his head practically opened up and a lot of blood and many more things came out.

Q   At this time, Mr. Zapruder, you heard the first shot were you able to see what reactions, if any, President Kennedy made at the time you heard this first shot? What did he do, sir, as you saw it?

A   As I said, he grabbed himself with his hand toward his chest or throat and leaned towards Jackie.

Q   At this time you heard the second shot, would you describe the reaction of President Kennedy as you saw them?

A   He leaned about the same way in falling towards Jacqueline, forward, down toward the bottom of the car.

Q   What happened at the time of the second shot, in regard to President Kennedy?

A   What happened—I don't understand.

Q   As you saw it, what happened at the time the second shot went off, in regard to President Kennedy? What did you see?

A   I thought I just described what I saw. You mean where it hit him?

Q   Yes.

A   I saw the head practically open up and blood and many other things, whatever it was, brains, just come out of his head.

Q   At the time when you heard these two shots, who was standing with you, if anybody?

A   One of my secretaries was right behind me.

Q   After the car passed under the underpass, what did you do?

A   I got off the abutment and walked towards my office. I was screaming "They shot him, they shot him." People asked me what happened, they probably didn't see what happened, they heard a shot, but didn't see what actually happened. I kept saying, "They killed him, they killed him," and I went to my office.

Q   When you got to your office. what, if anything, did you do with regard to your movie camera and films?

A   I had my secretary call either the police or the FBI, I don't remember which. She called somebody. Secret Service.

Q   After this, did you do anything with regard to your film? Did you go anywhere with your film?

A   Yes, sir, a patrol car came and took me down to the station where they were trying to develop films, but they hadn't got the facilities to develop colored film. We called the Eastman Kodak people and made

[SEVERAL PAGES MISSING]

MR. DYMOND:

      At this time we would like to traverse on the offer.

THE COURT:

      You may traverse.

BY MR. DYMOND:

Q   You say you were present when the copies of your film were made?

A   Yes, sir.

Q   Were you actually present in the room in which these copies were being made?

A   Yes, sir, I was in the processing room watching them process the film.

Q   Is the copy you have here today identical to the original or are there any plates missing out of this copy?

A   That would be hard for me to tell, sir.

THE COURT:

>I cannot hear the witness. What is it?

THE WITNESS:

>That would be hard for me to say. He asked me if there are any frames missing.

THE COURT:

>What is your answer?

THE WITNESS:

>I couldn't say.

BY MR. DYMOND:

Q   So you don't know whether it is a complete copy of the film you took on the 22nd of November?

A   Not if there are one or two frames missing, I couldn't tell you.

Q   Mr. Zapruder, when these copies were made, do I understand you ended up with an original and two copies of the film?

A   Yes, sir.

Q   You gave one copy to the Dallas Police Intelligence Section, is that correct?

A   Yes, sir.

Q   One copy to the FBI?

A   Correct.

Q   And one copy to *Life Magazine*?

A   Yes, sir.

Q   Where did you get the copy you have produced here in court today, if you disposed of all the copies?

A   I got them from Mr. Oser's office.

Q   In other words, this film has not been in your possession up until now, is that correct?

I haven't found any more carbons of this fascinating reading of the Clay Shaw trial. I am going sometime to the Supreme Court Building in the Quarter and determine if the originals are available. There are many conspiracies surrounding JFK's death. For instance, a bullet was found on President K's gurney which gave rise to magic bullet—it hit both, the President and the governor. All this information is to be researched and I will have enough for another story.

It has been a while since I wrote on these pages. Mia decided to move to the Quarter since the number of Christians in the area seems to be increasing. After doing a general inspection in Mia's vicinity, it was decided she would be an easy prey to snipers. The drizzle from the cloudy skies continues and I feel very insecure in this forever changing environment. Notwithstanding the reduction of population, I feel more threatened now than ever before: food scarcity and bellicose and brutal estrangers are appearing unexpectedly.

We went to the bunker and a couple of trips in the pick-up were sufficient to carry to the Quarter all those items that could be used by everyone: two gas generators, the very little food that was left, a number of tools, books, and other useful items. While I drove back to the Quarter, I thought that since the pick-up I was driving was the property of the Christians, perhaps I should discard it. After unloading everything, I drove the pick-up a few blocks from the Quarter and abandoned it. I went back to the Quarter and started a discussion about Mia's intense craving to be a mother: she wanted me to be the father or her child. I explained to her my condition and tried to calm her down with cunnilingus—again the role of coning linguist. I managed to delay her request for two weeks and then I submitted to her request: I showed her my penis stub. It was decided that, since at times I seemed to discharge sperms(?) when I became aroused at some stage during cunnilingus, we decided to transfer the discharge to her vagina. I also inserted my stub inside her vulva and remained insider her for long periods of time. We used an eye drop dispenser and several other forms of inserting my sperm in her vagina. This experimentation lasted about a year.

I decided to have a long discussion with Mia about life (or how it used to be) and changes in ethics and morals that the pandemic brought along for the survivors. I had advocated for the involvement of the seniors in her pregnancy to which she did not find acceptable. They would come to her place at midnight for three nights without indicating in which order they made their visit. The visits could be repeated until she was pregnant. She finally agreed and we have continued the visits for six months without success.

We, as a rational group, who are opposed to sects and organized religion, must find other people like us in order to save the world from Christians and other dooms-day sects. Now that Mia is part of the group, she accompanies me during my foray for food in other cities. It is becoming more difficult to find those warehouses where the grocery chains stored their supplies. The Quarter has become a fortress: All the entrances are now bordered up in addition to having them rigged with explosives. I suspect that's the reason we have not been attacked—yet.

I have been away from this journal for at least two years. We no longer travel at night for fear of an ambush so our forays to cities on the West and East coast are no longer viable. The experiment with the seniors was a failure. Mia would be impregnated after four or five months she would abort. It appears that the virus affects the unborn as well. I was hoping for the survival of a number of humans that would guide the planet into a sort of Eutopia, not to be confused with Utopia. If that were the case, these writings would have a "Hollywood Ending." Unfortunately, everything seems to indicate that it will not be the case.

As time passes (two or three years since I met Mia) a deep self-examination leads me to the conclusion I love Mia deeply. There had been very few instances in my happy life when I cursed the gods for my disability—this is one of them. Falling in love and not being able to perform sexually. I would give years of my life to be able to impregnate her. There are some lines in Steppenwolf in which Hesse portrays Maria and I think they are applicable to Mia:

> [. . .] she had been endowed with, and with her particular figure, her color, her hair, her voice, her skin, her temperament; and in employing every faculty, every curve and line and every softest modeling of her body to find responsive perceptions in her lovers and to conjure up in them an answering quickness of delight. What can I tell her? Do I know any reason for living? The truth is that I am not as desperate for living as she is in her short life. I never expected much from life, and I am amazed at how much life has given me. I feel sorry for Mia for she did not have a chance to live at all. I am neither a tragic hero nor a knight of faith.

I was hoping this story would have a different ending. The way things are developing, that will not be the case: Christians seem to have discovered New Orleans and have died as a result. We managed to neutralize many threats from the Christians, but they keep appearing.

ABOUT THE AUTHOR

Genaro J. Pérez holds a B.A. in English and Spanish from Louisiana State University in Baton Rouge and the M.A. and Ph.D. in Spanish and Portuguese from Tulane University. He is a retired Professor of Hispanic Literature at Texas Tech University. His primary scholarly interests include Twentieth and Twenty-First Centuries Spanish and Latin American literature as well as Chicano literature. Professor Pérez's academic publications include: *Formalist Elements in the Novels of Juan Goytisolo; La novelística de J. Leyva; La novela como burla/juego: siete experimentos novelescos de Gonzalo Torrente Ballester; La narrativa de Concha Alós: Texto, pretexto y contexto; Ortodoxia y heterodoxia de la novela policiaca hispana: Variaciones sobre el género negro; Rabelais, Bajtin, y formalismo en la narrativa de Sergio Pitol; Subversión y de(s)construcción de subgéneros en la narrativa de Rosa Montero; Misoginia, machismo y sadismo en la narrativa noir: El placer del texto*. His books of poems include: *Prosapoemas; Spanish Quarter Notes; French Quarter Cantos; Ten Lepers and Other Poems: Exorcising Academic Demons, Estelas en la mar: Cantos sentimentales; and Pandemic Prater: Pastel Palliatives*. His narrative includes: *The Memoirs of John Conde* and *French Quarter Tales*. He is Co-Editor and Co-Publisher of *Monographic Review/Revista monográfica* (Volumes I-XXVIII), and is Co-Editor of the journal *Dura*.

ACKNOWLEDGEMENTS

I want to thank my daughter Nicole T. Pérez for text layout and cover design.

Nicole Pérez is a Hispanic artist and designer from New Orleans. She worked as a corporate designer the last 30 years, while concurrently dedicated to her fine art practice and education from the School of the Art Institute of Chicago, where she received her MFA and BFA in painting and drawing. Nicole's work is devoted to revealing silhouetted moments of whimsy and wonder that one experiences when fully immersed in the here and now.

www.nicoleperez.net

Printed in the United States
by Baker & Taylor Publisher Services